~

Haley Connors is determined to make sure no one ruins her sister's wedding. But she suspects that the charming best man, Mike Sanderson, is the one behind all the little things that have been going wrong. Mike isn't anyone she intends to get to know better, and she has reason to believe he might not want to lose his best friend to marriage.

Mike Sanderson doesn't understand why the fiery older sister of the bride is so unfriendly. But since he's hell-bent on making sure his best buddy's wedding goes off without a hitch, he's going to have to keep a close eye on her. For all he knows, Haley might be the one messing with the wedding, and keeping an eye on the petite redhead won't be a hardship.

But when the incidents escalate to a dangerous level, Mike and Haley discover that teaming up to catch the culprit could have disastrous consequences... not just for the wedding or even for their lives but also for their hearts.

Readers of Book 1  *Inn on the coast of Maine w* *ur charac-*

D1534224

ters get a little help from the resident ghost and the mysterious stray tabby to whom newly widowed inn owner Ginny Flynn is determined not to get attached.

ANOTHER WISH

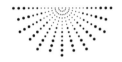

ANNIE DOBBS

MEREDITH SUMMERS

CHAPTER ONE

*H*aley Connors stood on the patio behind the historic Firefly Inn and stared out over the Atlantic Ocean in the distance. The warm breeze caressed her cheeks, and the lonely cry of seagulls echoed overhead. She licked her lips, tasting the salt from the water beyond, and smiled. She'd made the right decision, convincing her sister Kendra to have her wedding here in Maine. This was so much better and more cheerful than their sad, empty childhood home back in Nebraska.

From the corner of her eye, a flash of color caught her attention, and Haley turned to find that a section of paper lanterns the wedding planner, Stacy, had strung up for the party tomorrow night had fallen down. With a sigh, she walked over to fix them. Unfortunately, this wasn't the first mishap to occur during the wedding setup. In fact, a bunch of little things had gone wrong in one way or another since their arrival at the inn earlier that day with the rest of the wedding party—twelve of them in all—bride, groom, and five bridesmaids and five groomsmen.

After reattaching the string of lanterns, Haley hopped down off the chair she was standing on and took a seat at one of the small wrought iron tables. The troubles had started as soon as they'd arrived, in fact, with the broken zipper on Kendra's new luggage, causing the suitcase to open and her things to spill out all over the floor. Rachel, her sister's best friend and bridesmaid extraordinaire, had been there to help gather everything together, but still. Embarrassing. And somehow during their first night at the inn, several of the bridesmaids had lost either sunglasses or other personal items. Honestly, if Haley didn't know better, she'd think someone was deliberately trying to sabotage her sister's wedding.

Which was silly. She sighed and sat back. Who would want to hurt Kendra? She was seriously the sweetest, kindest, most wonderful kid sister ever. And yes, maybe Haley was a bit biased, but still. She owed it to Kendra to make sure this wedding was as successful as possible, especially after what had happened to their parents all those years ago.

Old sorrow squeezed Haley's chest, and she swallowed hard against the lump in her throat. The same thing always happened whenever she thought about the car accident that had taken Mom and Dad away from them. Haley had been just sixteen at the time and Kendra thirteen. It was just the two of them now and had been since the accident.

Even though their grandmother had taken them in, Haley had all but raised Kendra, feeling it was her responsibility to fill that parental role for her sister since it was her fault their parents had died. Haley hadn't meant to argue with them that day, but she'd been a stubborn teen and determined to gain her independence. Boy, had she gotten it all right. Twelve years on and she still carried the burden of responsibility every single day.

She sniffled and tipped her head back toward the sunlight streaming down from above. Being here was good, away from all that pain and guilt. Her only regret was letting Kendra talk her into making the wedding celebration a five-day extravaganza with their friends. Not that Haley didn't deserve a vacation. In fact, she couldn't remember the last time she'd taken time off just to enjoy life. But then, that was her penance for her sins.

Since their parents' passing, she'd become the caretaker, the responsible one who ensured everything in Kendra's life went to plan. And if Haley's own life took a back seat because of it, well, it was no more than she deserved.

A strong breeze gusted off the sea, making the fallen string of lights flap loose again. Haley stood and moved to the chair against the wall. Maybe if she secured them higher and tighter, they might stay put. She grabbed the string then kicked off her flip-flops, climbing up on the wobbly wrought iron chair, the metal cold against the pads of her feet as she strained her five-foot frame as far as she could go. There were times when being vertically challenged was a real pain in the butt.

She reminded herself to stop complaining. She was in a gorgeous place on the Maine coast, surrounded by their friends, and life was good. At least that's what Kendra had said on the ride over to the inn from the airport. Leave it to her baby sister to always look for the positive in any situation.

And as maid of honor, it was Haley's job to support Kendra's moods and wishes during this most special time of her life. Even if those wishes were a bit more nontraditional than conservative Haley would've picked for her own nuptials. From the decadent week-long stay here at the inn to the itinerary for the reception, it all reflected Kendra's unique point of view. It all cost a pretty penny too, but Kendra's fiancé could afford it. One of the perks of being from a prominent family of doctors as well as a rising-star pediatric intern at Sioux Falls General Hospital himself.

Haley strained higher on her tiptoes to reach the next higher hook fixed into the side of the building in order to secure the lights, one hand pressed to the side of the inn to keep her balance. She should be used to it by now. Back home, she was always having to get a step stool to even reach the top shelves in her kitchen. People had teased her about her shortness her whole life, or at least it seemed that way. Not that five feet was abnormally little, but still. The Cornhusker State seemed to grow its kids bigger and taller than the rest. Maybe it was all that farm work. She shrugged. Whatever the reason, Haley had grown up different than the other kids, and she didn't appreciate people remarking on her petite size or calling her cute and tiny.

Another gust of wind whistled past, and her chair wobbled precariously. Haley had just gasped and pressed closer to the clapboard wall to steady herself when something warm and solid came up behind her, surrounding her with strength and security and steadying her chair against the wind.

"Be careful there, little lady," a gruff male voice said, the tone laced with amusement. "Can't afford to have one of our own go down now. What are you doing up there anyway?"

Ugh. Mike Sanderson. Jared's best friend and best man for the wedding.

Scowling at his choice of description, Haley looked back over her shoulder to see the tall, blond playboy grinning up at her with that irritatingly gorgeous, cocky smile of his. "These lanterns came unhooked, so I'm putting them back up. What did it look like I was doing? Tap dancing?"

He snorted good-naturedly at her sarcasm and took the string from her hand, his strong fingers brushing hers and sending unexpected zings of awareness through her system. Mike reached past her and tied the string around the high hook like it was easy-peasey.

Her unaccountable annoyance growing by the second, Haley leaned her hip against the wall to put a bit more distance between them and crossed her arms, staring down at the enigmatic ex-soldier. From his muscular build to his six-foot-five height, the guy screamed Special Forces power—which is where he had served in the Army alongside Jared, from what she'd heard anyway.

Honestly, she really didn't know most of the wedding party that well. Because of their careers, she and Kendra now lived nearly two hundred miles apart, with Haley staying in their hometown of Omaha to teach grade school, while Kendra had moved to Sioux Falls, South

Dakota, after college to pursue her nursing career. In truth, before this trip, Haley had only met her sister's fiancé, Jared Murphy, a few times and knew little about him other than that he had gone to medical school after the military and was on a career path to become a surgeon who specialized in children born with facial deformities. Also, some of Kendra's friends had mentioned him having a bit of a playboy reputation before settling down with Kendra.

Rachel Wickham, in particular, had filled in a lot of blanks for Haley on their long plane ride to Maine. Rachel's family was from Omaha too, and she'd gone all through school with Kendra. They'd even roomed together in the dorms at the University of Nebraska. After graduation, Rachel had moved to South Dakota and gotten a job in the NICU at Sioux Falls General Hospital. From what Haley remembered, it had been Rachel who'd called Kendra about the opening for a surgical nurse in the pediatric department, where her sister and Jared had met and eventually fallen in love.

"All done," Mike said, holding out his hand to help Haley down. "You should've asked me to help you sooner. I'm just kicking around, waiting for whatever activity the girls have planned for us to start next."

Haley ignored his helping hand, and the disturbing tingles of awareness that would no doubt go along with it, and climbed off the chair herself then moved it back beside the table where it belonged. She was a stickler for neatness. Had to be with a classroom full of ten- and eleven-year-old maniacs running around. "Thank you, though I didn't need help. I was doing perfectly fine on my own before you showed up. Almost had it taken care of."

"All right then," he said, holding his hands up and backing away slightly. "No need to get snippy. Sorry. Didn't mean to get you all riled up."

Haley gave him a flat stare as she took her seat once more. She wasn't usually so prickly. Far from it in fact. Most of the folks who knew her in Omaha always commented on what a sweet, nice, kind person she was and what a shame it was she was still single.

But there was something about Mike Sanderson that had all her warning bells ringing. Maybe it was his affable, laid-back approach to everything that set her OCD tendencies on high alert. Maybe it was his looming presence, always ready to step in and save the day like some kind of wonky, misplaced superhero. Maybe it was just his penetrating blue eyes and the way it seemed like he could see right through Haley's bravado to the insecure, shy girl she still was underneath.

She shook her head and stared out at the Atlantic again.

Whatever it was, it was getting on her last nerve.

For all she knew, Mike had been the one out here screwing around with the lanterns earlier, and that's why they'd fallen down. After all, Rachel had told her that Jared and Mike used to be pretty wild in their younger days, always pulling practical jokes and causing trouble —when they weren't womanizing their way through half the population of Sioux Falls.

She cast a sideways glance in Mike's direction, her manners demanding she invite him to sit with her at the table but her cantankerous side refusing to do so. Let him stand there for a while, feeling uncomfortable. That would teach him to be all polite and offer to help her with those stupid lights.

Haley just hoped Mike and Jared had gotten all of that past wildness out of their systems before Jared got married.

The waves below the cliff were choppier now, from the sound of it, and crashed harder against the rocks and beach below the inn. "You didn't rile me up, by the way. I just don't like being called short. Or being thought of as less than capable because I'm petite."

"Huh." He pulled out the chair across from her and sat, wincing slightly as he did so. The wince made her frown. So did the raised, white scars visible on his left forearm and neck.

9

Rachel had mentioned those, too, on the plane. War wounds, she'd said. Apparently, both Jared and Mike had been discharged from the Army under less-than-ideal circumstances. Based on whatever misconduct they'd been charged with while in service to their country and the injuries that had resulted, Mike had spent several months in a field hospital, healing for pretty severe burns.

Rachel hadn't offered any specific details about the incident that had gotten them booted out of the military, and Haley wasn't about to ask at this point. After all, she barely knew Mike. And even though one little part of her kept nagging that she might make an effort to get to know him better—if only to be polite and have the wedding run smoothly—the rest of her had the urge to run in the opposite direction.

But there was something off about Mike. He seemed awfully interested in all the wedding preparations. That didn't seem like any guy she knew. What if he was jealous of his best friend or didn't like having a girlfriend horn in on what had been a two-person gig up to this point, and his interest wasn't in helping but in hindering?

"Well," Mike continued, "I obviously don't know anything about being short." The tips of his crew-cut hair sparkled with gold in the sunshine, and his deep blue gaze was narrowed on her, his smile self-deprecating.

"But I do know about not wanting people to notice your differences and about being thought of as less than capable because of them." He stared out to sea for a moment, then bowed his head. "That was never my intent, and I'm sorry if I made you feel that way."

And now didn't she just feel like a total jerk. Why did he have to go and be so charming and gallant and handsome? Haley exhaled slowly, her heart melting toward him a little as she stared down at the bright-pink polish on the nails of her bare toes. All the bridesmaids had gotten the same color, to match their dresses. Much as she didn't want to get closer to this man, she didn't want to be adversarial either. She didn't want any negative undercurrents to ruin things for Kendra. "I'm sorry too. I might have overreacted slightly."

"No." She glanced up at his sarcastic tone and found his grin contagious.

"Yeah." Haley smiled back, unable to help herself. "I've been known to do that."

Mike sat across from Kendra's older sister, a bit perplexed. He wasn't sure exactly what he'd expected Haley Connors to be like, but this woman wasn't it. Where Kendra had dark-brown, nearly black hair and wide blue eyes, Haley had coppery red hair and hazel eyes. Where Kendra was taller, just a few inches shorter than Jared's five-eleven, Haley barely came up to Mike's mid-chest. And where Kendra was outgoing and friendly and fun loving, Haley seemed quiet and reserved and serious beyond her twenty-eight years. As if she bore the responsibilities of the world on her petite shoulders.

He felt bad she'd been insulted by his words earlier. He hadn't meant them that way. It was just an expression, a charming line. Though apparently his charm didn't work on Haley.

He'd spoken from the heart when he'd said he understood her need to be seen as competent and more than her weaknesses. Hell, ever since that accident when he'd been stationed over in Mosul, he lived each day knowing most people only saw his scars and his limp and never looked past them.

Even in his job as a pharmaceutical rep, people still stared at his shuffling gait when he walked into the offices. Most days he didn't let it bother him, but there were still times when things got him down. Especially lately, with his best bud getting married. He'd always wanted to have a family of his own someday, and the older he got, the more pressing the need became, but that would probably never happen for him.

He was tired of being single and alone all the time,

but he knew his scars didn't help matters. Women weren't attracted to him anymore like they used to be. Even right now, Haley had averted her gaze to stare at the water rather than look at his disfigurements. Honestly, there were days he couldn't even stand the sight of himself in the mirror, so he couldn't blame her.

Still, he felt a compelling need to get Haley to like him for some reason, even though he'd only just met her. So he focused on what she'd said about the lanterns instead.

While Haley stared at the ocean, Mike stared at her. She really was stunning, in a more subdued way than Kendra. Her features were delicate, just like the rest of her, and her soft, pink lips all but begged a man to lean in and kiss her. Not that Mike was going to do that. Nope. He coughed to clear the sudden constriction in his throat and shifted his focus to her long, tanned legs and her cute little feet with their pink-painted toenails. He suddenly wondered if she were ticklish and how nice her laugh would sound if he dared to find out.

The bushes nearby rustled, and a small orange tabby cat darted out of the nearby gardens and wound around his ankles, purring loudly. Mike bent to pet it, smiling again. He loved animals. They didn't judge or care if you had a few scars or got kicked out of the military for what should've been considered an act of heroism or even if your best friend nearly died saving you. They just wanted love and affection and kindness, all of which he had to give in spades.

"So, you and Jared are best buds then, huh?" Haley asked, holding a hand over her eyes to shield them from the sun, which had cleared the trees behind him as she looked his way at last. "You've known each other a long time."

"Yep. We go all the way back to grade school together." He sat back as the cat moved on to sniff Haley's toes. "We're about as tight as they come."

"That's good. Loyalty is good." Haley bent to scratch the feline, and once more Mike was struck with how pretty she was.

Haley straightened and met his gaze, hers narrowed. "Listen, I don't want to be walking on eggshells this whole week, so I'm just going to say it. I don't know Jared that well, or you. But I've heard things about both of you that have me worried. And some strange things have been happening since we got here." She gestured toward the patio lanterns. "I want you to know I will do everything in my power to protect my sister, including telling her if I see anything that looks suspicious."

Mike's eyes narrowed. "What do you mean by suspicious?" He'd noticed some wonky stuff happening since their arrival, stuff coming up missing or broken, and had started to wonder himself. And the string holding those patio lights looked like it had been cut, not all the way but only three-quarters, as if maybe someone was hoping they'd fall down at the most inopportune time.

"There's been a few things that have happened since we arrived yesterday. Like my sister's brand-new luggage breaking and stuff going missing. It's all got me thinking someone might be messing with the wedding. And I won't let that happen."

Mike glanced back at the patio lights. "You think someone deliberately pulled those lights down?"

Haley shrugged. "Maybe."

Mike had wondered about that himself. He felt the same loyalty toward Jared that she felt toward her sister. And he felt the same need to put a stop to it if someone was trying to ruin things for his best bud. Not just because Mike was best man either, but because Jared was so happy now with Kendra, happier than Mike had ever seen him. Then there was the not-so-small fact that Mike owed Jared his life. Therefore, he made it his business to make sure this wedding was the best ceremony ever.

"I just want to make it clear that I'm not going to let anything stand in the way of my sister's happiness. Understand?"

Mike nodded, watching as she stood and slipped her

flip-flops back on then walked away, heading inside the inn's shadowy conservatory.

For a long while afterward, Mike sat alone on the patio, considering where things stood. It was clear Haley was passionate about the things she cared for, including Kendra. She was a good sister and friend too, worried about the wedding like she was. Loyalty was something he valued, even more so since returning Stateside, still recovering from his burns and injuries, only to have his then-girlfriend dump him without warning. His chest still squeezed at the pain of that breakup, even though it had been years now.

But if the vibes he was picking up from her were right and if she didn't approve of her sister's relationship with Jared, was it possible that passion could've turned into making sure her sister didn't marry a man she considered unworthy?

Could Haley have resorted to sabotaging her own sister's wedding? She'd been standing right here near the lanterns when he came out to the patio. Had she been putting them up or taking them down? But if she was the one messing with things, then why would she call attention to it by mentioning it to him? Maybe she figured it would make him act suspicious so she could blame these little mishaps on him. No, that would be really strange. Then again, he'd seen stranger things happen, like someone bombing a village when they knew kids and civilians were inside, just to take out a few allied soldiers on a goodwill mission...

Pulling himself back from dangerous territory, Mike leaned back in his chair and stretched out his stiff legs. Haley was right about one thing; someone was trying to mess with the wedding.

If Haley was somehow involved in the weird happenings surrounding her sister's wedding, then he might need to be a bit more vigilant himself, keep an eye on her. Strictly as a precaution, of course. After all, he took his best man duties very seriously. And that included making sure Jared's wedding went off without issues, no matter what Kendra's cute, fiery older sister might do to stop it.

irginia Flynn—known to most in Boulder Point, Maine, as Ginny and owner of the Firefly Inn—crouched in a small garden on the side of the partially restored inn she'd purchased with her late husband Donald, weeding around the new rosebushes she'd planted a month earlier. The place was now coming along nicely after a rocky first few months. She stopped to swipe her hand over her sweaty forehead and noticed a half-eaten dish of cat food nearby. Well, that was good. Her little stray had eaten, finally. At least something was going right around the place these days.

She'd not seen the little orange tabby for a while and thought that at last maybe he'd been adopted by someone nearby. That would have been good. The last thing Ginny wanted right now was to get too close to the tiny cat. She didn't need it depending on her, because everything that got close to her had a tendency to die. That was what had happened to her family. That was what had happened to her poor, beloved late husband Donald too.

So the cat came. It ate. It left again. Fine by her.

Sitting back on her heels, Ginny stared out across the yard to the ocean in the distance. Even though she didn't want a pet, she didn't want the poor little cat to starve either. A flash of movement caught her attention on the patio at the rear of the inn. Through the rosebushes, she spotted two of their new guests, Haley and Mike. They'd both been nice as could be during check-in, though she sensed a lingering sadness in each of them. The cause of Haley's sorrow she hadn't quite figured out yet, since Haley was cute as a button and smart as a whip. And only in her twenties too. Odd for such a vibrant young woman to carry such grief.

Mike, on the other hand, well, that poor man carried his scars on the outside. From his stiff manners and politeness, he had military written all over him. Her Donald had served in the Navy after high school, so she recognized an ex-serviceman when she saw one. She wasn't sure what exactly had caused those raised white welts all over his left arm and neck, and though he was still strikingly handsome and virile, she imagined he lived with that pain—both physical and emotional —each day.

Ginny gathered up her tools as quietly as she could while keeping an eye on the young couple. The two of them were sitting at one of the cute little antique wrought iron bistro tables she'd purchased in town last month and, judging from their sly looks and curt gestures, seemed to be having quite a conversation. And while they didn't seem to be overly friendly at the moment, wouldn't it be nice to have another romance start and blossom here at the inn?

Just a month prior, Ginny had witnessed love bloom between her new event planner, Stacy Brighton, and local caterer Reid Callahan. Those two had been hot and heavy during high school then lost touch for years before reuniting here at the inn after Stacy's father had passed away.

Young love was always so refreshing.

Love, period, was good for the soul. After all, she and her Donald had been married for thirty-six blissful years, until his unexpected death the previous year. At first, Ginny had been quite flummoxed, unsure what to do with herself, let alone the new inn she and her late husband had purchased here on the Maine coast to refurbish and run as a bed and breakfast, as they'd done with so many other properties previously. But then she'd settled in here in Boulder Point, made some friends, gotten involved in the renovations for this place, and gotten back on her feet again.

Now she couldn't imagine living anywhere else. Over the past month, she'd also found herself thinking about her Donald less and less too, which was good. Didn't do to dwell on the past and forget to live, as one of her favorite literary characters always said. Plus, there just wasn't much time for reflection these days when she was so busy with the inn.

Or rather with all the small things going *wrong* at the inn.

This Connor-Murphy wedding was the first big event her inn had hosted, and she really needed it to go off without a hitch. Word of mouth was incredibly important in the hospitality business, and a few bad reviews could sink a small venture like the Firefly Inn. Unfortunately, a few things had mysteriously gone awry as of late. Tiny mishaps like decorations falling down or floral arrangements being the wrong color or size or shape. Personal items turning up missing. None of these things in themselves were suspicious, but when combined... well, it seemed like too many of these things happening in such a short time.

All fixable, of course, but still. This event, and her inn, couldn't afford bad press. Businesses in the picturesque seaside village of Boulder Point, Maine, lived or died by the tourist trade, and it could only take one or two dissatisfied customers to ruin her reputation. Up until now, things had proceeded nicely.

If you didn't count Dooley, her resident ghost.

Ginny chuckled and finished spreading a fresh layer of mulch around the roots of the roses. When she'd first taken up residence here, the townsfolk of Boulder Point had been only too happy to regale her with all sorts of spooky stories about Dooley and his hauntings, but she hadn't really believed them.

At least, not until the time you actually heard his voice...

A slight shiver ran through her, and she shook it off, along with her own folly. Ghosts weren't real, and most likely Dooley was just a figment of her overactive, over-lonely imagination.

What would her Donald have thought of her talking to ghosts? She laughed. It had to have been the emotional stress of the inn opening, that was all. Still, she'd stopped moving around the antique salt and pepper shakers that had been in the inn when she'd bought it, just in case the ghostly voice that had requested she do so was actually real.

She shook clumps of soil from her trowel before heading back toward the decrepit toolshed in the back of the gardens. After this wedding was done, she really needed to call someone about repairing that shed or tearing it down and rebuilding it.

"Ginny?" Stacy said, poking her head around the side screen door, halting Ginny mid-trek. "Do you have a second to discuss some of the arrangements for the wedding this weekend?"

"I do." She grinned at seeing Stacy's radiant smile, feeling no small amount of pride in the other woman's happiness. Stacy had decided to move back to Boulder Point to be with Reid, and their relationship was going well. Of course, Ginny had known from the minute she'd seen the two of them together that they were meant for each other. It had just taken a little push to help them realize it themselves. "Let me just put these tools away and wash up. I'll meet you in the library in five minutes."

"Sounds perfect." Stacy walked back into the house, and Ginny continued on to the shed.

Once the tools were put away, she walked back to the house and proceeded down the hall to the tiny mudroom near the front entrance and washed her hands in the large stainless-steel sink there. After she'd dried her hands and checked her appearance in the mirror—same sleek white bob, same sparkling blue eyes—she headed to the old library at the back of the inn.

Stacy worked for her full time now, planning all the

events rapidly filling up their schedule. Her ever-organized wedding planner was waiting with paperwork scattered over the long wooden table in the middle of the room.

Ginny swiped a hand down her denim capris and gingham work shirt, wishing she'd had time to change before the meeting. Especially since Stacy looked fresh as a daisy in her crisp white shirt and pink floral skirt, her hair slicked back into a neat ponytail and her makeup done to perfection, as always. She'd spent the past several years working in the corporate world of Columbus, Ohio, and it showed in her wardrobe and grooming.

"How are the roses coming along?" Stacy asked, smiling as Ginny entered.

"Good. I think they're finally taking root." Ginny took a seat beside Stacy at the table. "Though I think that has more to do with Emery than with me."

Emery Santos was the new gardener Ginny had hired to whip the grounds and landscaping around the inn into shape. Even though Emery had been there a few weeks, Ginny still liked to dig in the dirt a bit herself. Nice girl and impeccable references, though she'd wondered how a gal of her credentials had ever ended up in the tiny village of Boulder Point. After all, Emery had a master's degree in horticulture, for goodness' sake.

"Good," Stacy said, smiling. "I'm glad she's working

out. Once things calm down around here, I'd love to get to know her better. It's just always so busy these days. And the few times our paths do cross during the week, she always seems to keep to herself."

"Yes. She's very quiet. Doesn't say much to me either, and I'm her boss." Ginny laughed. "But I'm working on getting her to open up a bit more. She's such a pretty thing, and smart too, with an advanced degree like that. There's more to her story. I can sense it."

"Well, if anyone can draw her out of her shell, it's you." Stacy handed her the final contracts from Reid's catering service. They went over the bride and groom's meal selections and double-checked the headcounts for the guests as well as the wine and beverage costs and soon lost themselves in the thrills of making someone else's dreams come true.

Sometime later, the screen door banged closed on the side of the house, and Emery tromped down the hallway in her khaki cargo shorts and T-shirt, heavy black work boots on her feet, to stand in the library door—a shovel in one hand and a bucket in the other, her gaze wary as she watched the two women work at the table. Her tanned skin and coal-black hair shone, in contrast to her usual uniform. "I've finished clearing the gardens in the back of the house, ma'am. Sorry it took longer than usual. A few of the guests came out, and I didn't want to intrude in their business. I'll finish the side gardens tomorrow, if that's all right with you."

"That's fine." Ginny smiled. Emery was always so serious, which stood in sharp contrast to her dark, soulful eyes and full pink lips. She was slim and on the shorter side and seemed to walk with her shoulders slumped, as if she wanted to draw the least attention to herself possible, but there was no hiding her natural beauty. She looked like a young Delores Del Rio, and Ginny couldn't help but wonder why a woman would try to hide her obvious assets. Still, in an effort to make the girl feel more comfortable, she didn't mention any of that. Instead, she tried to elicit a smile from Emery. "Do you have plans for your afternoon off? Meeting someone perhaps?"

"Yeah," Stacy joined in, grinning. "Got a hot date?"

"What?" Emery's eyes widened, and the color drained from her cheeks, her tone wary. "No. Not at all. Why would you think that?"

"Oh, well, I was just teasing," Stacy said. "I'm sorry."

Ginny narrowed her gaze on the young gardener. From the alarm in Emery's tone and her overreaction to what had obviously been good-natured ribbing, maybe she *was* meeting someone this afternoon and didn't want anyone to know. Or maybe she'd met someone in the past and things hadn't gone well. Either way, whatever Emery Santos was doing on her afternoon off from the inn was still a mystery. "It's fine, Emery. Stacy was just joking. You have a nice afternoon off and we'll see you tomorrow, yes?"

"Yes, ma'am." Emery gave a curt nod and walked away, leaving Stacy and Ginny to stare after her.

"Well, that was weird," Stacy said, shaking her head.

"Yes, it was." Ginny exhaled slowly, still staring after Emery's form retreating down the hallway. "And all the more reason for me to find out what's going on inside the head of that poor girl. If anyone needs a friend to talk to around here, it's Emery."

CHAPTER THREE

*A*fter her run-in with Mike Sanderson on the patio, Haley decided to head upstairs to make sure Kendra was settling in okay. Their rooms were the two best rooms in the inn, situated next door to each other, facing the ocean. The other bridesmaids had smaller rooms in the back near the back stairs, but even those rooms still had a nice view of the gardens and large field on the side of the house.

She walked past the dining room and down the hall toward the library, where she spotted the inn's owner, Ginny, and the wedding planner, Stacy, working. Haley stepped aside to allow the somewhat surly gardener to pass then waved as she passed the library, noting all the lovely old candle holders scattered over every available surface. All the rooms and spaces downstairs in the inn were dotted with them, just as she'd asked. They'd be lit on the day of her sister's wedding, and if things went to plan, the effect would be stunning.

She climbed the stairs up to the second floor, past the landing and the gorgeous oval window overlooking the meadow on the side of the inn, then headed straight for Kendra's door. She knocked before walking on in. "Hey, sis. How's the unpacking going?"

"Okay, I think." Kendra stuffed a stack of underwear and socks into the drawer of the refurbished, white-washed dresser against the wall. All the rooms at the inn seemed to have a shabby-chic vibe to them that suited the area perfectly. Her sister's wedding dress hung on a hook beside the dresser, the garment bag open to allow the lace and beading a chance to breathe after being cooped up in the cargo hold of the plane for the four-and-a-half-hour plane ride there.

"How about you?" Kendra asked, stowing her now-empty suitcase under the bed. "You all settled in?"

"Yep. But I didn't bring nearly as much stuff as you."

"Of course not." Kendra winked. "Always the responsible one."

"Always." Haley kicked off her flip-flops again and stretched out on the window seat overlooking the cliffs at the back of the inn. She had the same type of setup in her room and looked forward to reading there later after everyone else had gone to bed. "I was down on the patio a little while ago and ran into Mike."

"Yeah?" Kendra opened the door of the robin's-egg-blue antique armoire and grabbed several hangers from inside, her expression dubious. "How'd that go?"

"Fine." She gave her sister an irritated look. "I can be civil to the guy, even if I don't trust him."

"Seriously, sis. You need to stop worrying so much. Mike's a good guy." Kendra snorted as she hung up her clothes. "Honorable, loyal, kind. I wish you two got along better. I think you could really be good together."

"Whoa." Haley straightened. "I don't know where that idea came from, but you can get it out of your head right now."

She crossed her arms, remembering Mike's warm smile and the tingles of electric awareness that had sizzled up her arm when he'd touched her. Sure, he was hot, but she wasn't looking for a relationship, especially with a man with his past. A man who could be behind the rash of mistakes around here for all she knew. She shook her head, frowning. "I'm just looking to get through this wedding without any problems. Not looking for a date."

"What?" Kendra gave her an innocent look, batting her pretty blue eyes. "I wasn't planning anything. Promise."

"Sure you weren't." Haley wasn't convinced. "So, are we heading down to the beach?"

"Definitely."

As they talked, Kendra finished hanging up her clothes in the closet then grabbed a tote bag from one of the dresser drawers and began shoving items into it—beach towels, sunscreen, sunglasses, her iPod and earphones, a book to read. Haley had the same bag packed in her room and planned to stop and get it on their way out.

"Don't forget your EpiPen," Haley said. Kendra was allergic to bees and wasps and had deathly reactions if stung. Summer was prime time for bee attacks.

"Yes, Mother." Her sister rolled her eyes affectionately as she went in the attached bathroom to grab her device.

At the title, Haley's heart pinched with grief and guilt. Truth was, she had taken on the role after their parents had died. Then again, their deaths were her fault, so it was the least she could do. She'd often wondered over the years, if she hadn't argued with their mom and distracted their dad before they'd left on their trip, would they still be alive? Would they be here now, at the inn, to see their baby girl get married?

Tears burned the back of Haley's eyes, and she

blinked hard to keep them at bay. If only she could take back her hateful words and angry spite. If only...

"Right. I'm ready," Kendra said, slinging her bag over her shoulder. "Have you seen Rachel or the other bridesmaids yet?"

"No. Not yet. I think Rachel and Simone were making sandwiches for the beach." Truthfully, Haley had gotten more than enough time with chatty Rachel on the trip here to last her a lifetime, but the woman was her sister's best friend, and thus Haley would tolerate her for the week. The other bridesmaids were quiet by comparison, three nurses who worked with Kendra at the hospital—Beth, Georgia, and Simone.

With a sigh, Haley pushed to her feet and slid on her flip-flops again before following her sister to the door. "I need to change and grab my bag before we head down."

They walked next door into Haley's room, which was the mirror opposite of Kendra's. Same restored antique furniture, same queen-sized brass bed, same antique armoire for a closet, same attached bath. Some of the other rooms had a shared bathroom in the hall, which she supposed was fine for the guys on the other side of the inn. Men were such different creatures altogether. They wouldn't mind sharing, but for the ladies, having quality mirror time this week was essential. In fact, on the day of the wedding ceremony, they would all probably be holed up in their rooms for hours getting their hair and makeup just perfect.

Haley changed, then grabbed her tote and her sunglasses from the top of her dresser then walked back out into the hall to join Kendra.

"So, explain to me again why you don't like Mike?" Kendra asked as they descended the stairs to the first floor.

"It's not that I don't like him, I just don't trust him."

"Right. Because that's so much better," Kendra teased as they pushed out the front door and onto the sunlit wraparound porch. "Why don't you trust him? You just met the poor guy."

"I've heard things, that's all. About his wild past." Haley slid her sunglasses into place as they headed down to the path to the back gardens. A gate opened near the cliff, and a set of weather-worn wooden stairs led down to the beach. "I don't know. It just seemed like he was hiding something when I talked to him earlier."

"Hiding something?" Kendra gave her a look, the salty sea breeze blowing her hair into her face. She pressed a hand to the sunhat on her head and laughed. "Did you ever stop to think he might be uncomfortable around you? Miss prim and proper and perfect?"

"I am not prim or proper. And God help us all if I'm perfect." Haley inhaled deeply, savoring the sun warming her skin and the sweet smell of roses. "Blame your friend Rachel. She was the one who filled me in on his and Jared's sordid pasts on the plane ride over. She also told me about their discharge from the Army. I don't know. Seems like he and Jared both were quite the troublemakers back in the day. And who knows what they were up to to get that 'other than honorable conditions' discharge." She shrugged. "If all that's still going on, I can't imagine Mike would be too pleased about losing his partner in crime to you."

"Trust me, Jared's playboy days are far behind him." Kendra chuckled. "And I suspect Mike's are too. There's a lot more to him than meets the eye, sis. He's changed a lot since his days in the Army. Both of the guys have. And whatever happened to get them in trouble also seemed to set them on a new path in life. Honestly, these days, Mike's one of the sweetest, kindest, most thoughtful guys I know."

"Hmm." Much as she wanted to believe her sister, Haley still wasn't convinced. About either man. She really wanted to believe Jared had changed his ways, for Kendra's sake, and wanted to believe he was a good man, because her sister was head-over-heels in love with him. But the past was a hard thing to leave behind. "What exactly happened to get them that questionable discharge?"

"Don't know." Kendra shook her head as they exited the gardens through the gate in the back and headed over the short distance of flat, smooth rocks to the cliff's edge and the steep,

rickety stairs leading to the beach below. "Neither of the guys ever talks about it, and the few times I've brought it up, Jared always changes the subject fast."

Haley clutched the wooden railings on either side of her and turned that information over in her head. Could that discharge have something to do with why Mike might want to sabotage his best friend's wedding? Was there some secret he was afraid Jared might share with his new wife that Mike didn't want leaked? The more she considered the idea, the more interesting it became.

Then again, her previous suspicion that Mike didn't want a pesky wife to stand in the way of the fun with his old buddy seemed more plausible. Either way, she was going to keep a close eye out to make sure nothing more went wrong.

"Hey," Kendra said once they reached the bottom of the steps, jarring Haley out of her thoughts. "It's so gorgeous here, isn't it?"

"Yeah, it is." They kicked off their shoes, and warm sand squished through Haley's toes as they walked down the beach to join the rest of their wedding party, who were already camped out ahead.

"Why so serious, sis?" Kendra asked, tilting her head slightly.

"What?" Haley glanced over at her sister and forced a smile. "I'm okay."

"Listen, I know now's probably not the time to say this, but I want to thank you for taking such good care of me all these years." They stopped, and Kendra took her hands, leaning in to kiss Haley's cheek. "I know you did it partly because you felt responsible for me after Mom and Dad died, but I want you to know how much I appreciate it and to let you know you're free now. You have to stop blaming yourself for Mom and Dad's accident. It wasn't your fault. And I've got Jared now. But I want you to find someone too, sis. Someone who makes you as happy as Jared makes me. Someone to love you for the rest of your life. You deserve it, Haley."

Chest squeezing with love, Haley embraced her baby sister tightly. "You don't have to thank me. Ever. I love you more than life itself, Keni girl. All I've ever wanted was for you to be happy. And if Jared's the one, then I'll love him too. Just give me some time. It's a big change for me too. And please promise me that you'll cherish every moment you have with him. We know only too well how love can be snatched away so fast, and I never want to see that happen to you again, okay?"

They both sniffled, and Haley blinked back tears

once more. After blowing their noses and having a good laugh at their blubbering on the beach in front of everyone, the sisters held hands as they walked over to join the rest of the wedding party.

Haley's traitorous eyes zoned in on Mike right away, all tanned and toned and looking far too handsome than should be allowed for a man in a T-shirt and board shorts. Kendra must've noticed her staring too, since she leaned in to whisper, "Seriously. Go talk to him, Haley. You two have a lot more in common than you think. Just promise me you'll really make an effort to take some time today to get to know him."

"I don't know," Haley said, frowning. "He's not my usual type." Then again, it might be a good idea to stick close to him just in case he was the one behind all the mishaps. He wouldn't be able to do anything to sabotage the wedding in her presence.

"Exactly." Kendra nudged shoulders with her. "That's what makes him so great. He's not buttoned up and buttoned down. He doesn't spend all day with his nose stuck in a book or a bank account. Mike's a rugged outdoorsman. He's a guy's guy. He's special. And so are you."

They joined the rest of their crowd and ended up in the spot close to where Jared and Mike were sitting. Haley eyed the boys' disorganized pile of stuff as she put her towel neatly on the sand. Mike glanced over and caught her eye, raising his hand in greeting before Haley looked away fast, her cheeks heating, and not from the sun.

He's a guy's guy. He's special...

As Haley settled in on her towel in between Simone and Kendra, she couldn't seem to keep her sister's words from looping over and over again in her head. Mike was definitely a man, no doubt about that. Even through the thin cotton fabric of his T-shirt, she could see the lines of his muscled arms and trim chest, and honestly, he was built like a Greek statue. And even his scars somehow only made him more intriguing and handsome to her.

Jared grabbed a volleyball and headed down the beach. "Who wants to play?"

Mike jumped up to join him, and Haley noticed he looked as good from the back as he did from the front.

But the question lingered in her mind—what if Mike wasn't really as honorable and kind as Kendra seemed to think he was?

The jury was still out for her on the guy, that was for sure.

"So, how do you think it's going so far?" Jared asked before spiking the ball to Mike over the sagging volleyball net they'd strung up in the sand. Everyone else was taking their sweet time in joining in, so it was just the two of them. "You and Kendra's sister getting along okay?"

"Fine." Mike slapped the ball back to his buddy. The stinging against his palm felt good, distracting him from the two women who'd just arrived and the weight of Haley's stare, which he felt even though he wasn't looking at her. "We talked briefly on the patio earlier."

"And?" Jared collected the ball from where it had rolled wide then jogged back to stand across the net from Mike. The sun had been beating down on them relentlessly for the last hour or so, and he could feel his scars tightening up down the side of his neck and on his arm despite his T-shirt.

He'd have to take a break soon to put on more sunscreen. Add that to the list of things nobody told you about burn injuries. Scar tissue sunburned way more quickly than normal skin. Still, that wasn't the only reason he'd covered up to come down here. He might be gaining more confidence in his new appearance each day, but that didn't mean anyone else needed to be subjected to his puckered skin and raw red patches.

"And nothing, man." Mike scoffed, giving the groom-to-be an annoyed stare. "Are we gonna play volleyball or talk all day like a couple of girls?"

Teams formed, and soon they shot the ball back and forth for several minutes, Jared landing a nice slam dunk over the net, causing Mike to dive for it and end up with a face full of sand. Everyone had a good laugh about it, but Jared had been quick to rush over to Mike's side to lend him a helping hand while the rest of them retreated to their towels or ran into the cold surf to cool off.

"It's good to see you happy again, bud," Jared said, slapping Mike on the back once he was on his feet again. "You've been too serious since we came back from Mosul."

"Gee, I wonder why." Mike gave him a look then shook his head to try and get some of the sand out of his hair. "An unexpected discharge and an extended hospital stay will do that to a guy. Sorry I wasn't a laugh riot."

"You know what I mean." Jared tossed him the volleyball, his gaze drifting to his fiancée sitting under an umbrella a few feet away. Mike was happy for them. He really was. Kendra had saved Jared's life just as surely as Jared had saved his the day they'd snuck into that remote Iraqi village against their CO's orders to take medicine to a kid who'd needed it.

It figured that no good deed would go unpunished over there, and Jared had ended up pulling Mike out of the wreckage of a bombed-out, burning hut after the kid's village had been attacked by rebels.

To this day, if Mike closed his eyes long enough, he could still feel the sting of flames licking his skin, could still hear the desperate cries for help from villagers trapped inside just like he'd been, could still taste the bitterness of ash from the fire clogging his mouth and nose.

No matter that they'd both gotten an other-than-honorable-conditions discharge for sneaking out; that was nothing compared to the horror of those moments. Not in a million years. He took a deep breath and shook off the shroud of the past.

A seagull swooped low overhead, its plaintive cry suiting his pensive mood.

He swiped a hand over his sweaty, gritty face then slid his sunglasses back on, squinting over at the prim Miss Haley Connors. She seemed the opposite of her fun-loving sister in many ways, and not just physical. Though he'd only spent a brief amount of time with her earlier, she'd seemed wound up so tight that something was about to break. He couldn't help wondering exactly what it was that had her so torn and twisted. Couldn't help wondering too if that controlling nature of hers might've taken a turn for the dark side where her sister and Jared were concerned.

From her comments earlier, he'd gotten the impression she was well aware of his and Jared's previous wild reputations and didn't approve. And could her disapproval and her need to protect her sister extend to sabotaging the wedding? After all, no one would suspect the maid of honor of such dastardly deeds, right?

Frowning, he glanced between Jared and Haley. "How well do you know Kendra's sister?"

Jared shrugged, his grin widening. "Not that well. Why? You interested?"

"Yes. But not that way." *Liar.* Truth was, he kind of *was* interested in Haley that way, but what would a pretty girl like her see in a scarred-up guy like him? Nothing, that's what. Even his own girlfriend of five years hadn't wanted to have anything to do with him after she saw his scars. And anyway, Haley could be the person behind all these little incidents that had been happening, and if she was *that* kind of person, he definitely wasn't interested. Mike gave his buddy a flat expression. "When I was out on the patio before, someone had knocked down those lights Kendra put up again."

"Really?" Jared scrunched his nose, which was growing more pink by the second. "That's weird."

"Yeah. I thought so too."

"Are you sure it wasn't just the wind? It's pretty breezy on top of the cliffs."

"No. Based on where the hook was to attach them, it couldn't have been the wind. Too close to the building." Mike watched as Haley fussed with her towel then her sunhat, then pulled off her glittering green T-shirt to reveal a neon-pink bikini she seemed to think passed for a swimsuit. Feeling a sudden rush of inappropriate heat zoom through his body, Mike coughed to clear the sudden constriction from his throat and ignored the knowing glance Jared cast his way. Todd, one of the other groomsmen, was looking at Haley too, and Mike felt a rush of... jealousy? No way. He had bigger fish to fry. "Anyway, from what I could tell, the string holding those lanterns up had been cut. The ends were frayed. Looked deliberate to me."

"Hmm." The two men stared at the women sitting on the beach like a flock of exotic birds. Jared tucked the volleyball under his arm and frowned. "Wait. You don't think Haley had something to do with it, do you?"

Mike just shrugged in response.

"Nah, man. No way. She and Kendra are too close. Haley dotes on her."

"Maybe that's why she did it. Maybe Haley doesn't like the idea of her sister getting married. Who would she take care of if Kendra had a husband? She's not married or living with anyone, right? No kids or man of her own, so if she loses Kendra, what's she got left?"

Jared scoffed. "Sorry, but you're crazy, buddy. Some lanterns fell down. A string broke. Big deal. Hardly means anybody's out to destroy our ceremony." He laughed and clapped Mike on the shoulder. "I think maybe it's been too long since you dated somebody seriously, man. Too many one-nighters under your belt. Maybe you should focus on getting yourself a steady girlfriend of your own and quit worrying about my life so much."

"Right. Sure." Mike sighed and rolled his stiff neck, his tone sarcastic. "Because my last relationship worked out so well."

"Hey, forget that loser, Courtney. She was a self-absorbed idiot who didn't care about anybody but herself. She didn't deserve you, man."

Mike chuckled and shook his head. "Whatever, man. I don't want to get involved right now anyway. I travel too much with my job, and it's hard to keep a relationship going like that. Now get over there to Kendra before she breaks her wrist waving at you to get your attention."

"Right. Duty calls." Jared laughed and tossed him the volleyball before sprinting over to pull Kendra from her chair and kiss her soundly. Whoops and hollers sounded from the rest of the wedding party gathered on the beach, and Mike couldn't help but smile.

His best bud had finally found the girl of his dreams and was settling down to start a new life and family with the woman he loved. Mike started trekking back to where his towel sat near Jared's on the sand. Haley had arranged herself so she was as far away from him as possible. The woman wanted to avoid him, it seemed, which only made him more curious about her. All the more reason for him to discover who'd messed with those lanterns and put a stop to that craziness before it got out of hand.

CHAPTER FOUR

*H*aley watched Mike walk back to their group and plop down on his towel. He was a few towels away from her but still close enough to her for her to see fine grains of sand clinging to his skin and smell the faint coconut scent of the sunscreen he was slathering on his arms. One of the groomsmen made a joke she didn't quite catch, and the low hum of Mike's voice in response shivered over her like a physical caress.

Thankfully, Haley's oversized dark shades kept anyone from seeing where her attention was focused. It was better if he didn't know she was watching him. Maybe he'd slip up, and she could catch him in the act of trying to ruin the wedding.

She shook herself out of her haze and squinted over at the three other guys in the wedding party—Todd,

Mark, and Aaron—who all worked at the hospital with Jared. Todd and Aaron were both ER physicians, and Mark worked in administration. All of them were smack talking about the wimpy volleyball skills they'd just displayed.

"Anybody hungry?" Rachel asked, opening the large, rolling cooler the guys had brought down earlier. "We made a bunch of sandwiches, and the cook at the inn threw in some goodies." She started pulling out baggies and bottles and plates and napkins, passing them around to everyone.

"Looks like we've got ham and turkey and cheese..." Rachel pulled out a mushy-looking sandwich. "... and peanut butter, banana, and honey. This one's yours, Mike." She tossed the mushy sandwich to Mike, and Haley noticed a look pass between them. What was that about?

The cook, Maisie, had made peanut butter cookies, and Rachel passed those around. Haley settled back on her towel and opened her own baggie containing a turkey sandwich.

"Anybody want to go swimming after?" Rachel asked, pulling her sandwich out and tossing the baggie down on the blanket she shared with Kendra. Haley frowned at the bag. Was that the same thing Mike was eating? Was that why they'd shared a look? Because they ate the same sandwich, or was there more to it? Rachel continued, "The tide's starting to come in, and the inn owner told me the waves will be really high."

"We need to wait a half hour after eating," Simone said.

Rachel made a face. "That's not really true. Well, sort of, but..."

Ignoring Rachel's constant chatter, Haley dug into her food, not realizing until then how hungry she was. She'd missed breakfast that morning.

"I think we could sunbathe for a little while then go in," Kendra said, handing half of her ham-and-cheese sandwich to Jared. "It can't hurt, right?"

"I suppose." Rachel turned her attention back to flirting with Todd and Aaron, who were both still single. Mark had been married for going on five years, he'd said. Haley hadn't met his wife yet, as she couldn't come for the whole week, but she'd be joining them on the day of the wedding along with most of the others from the small list of invited guests. They all seemed like nice enough guys, if a bit bland for Haley's taste. She'd always gone for the more complex, deeper kind of man. Her glance slid toward Mike again before she forced it away.

What was she thinking? He could be the enemy. And besides, she knew all too well that these kinds of flings only ended in heartbreak. She'd learned at a young age not to let her feelings run amok; one never knew when loved ones could be snatched away at a moment's notice.

Besides, she was not in the market for a man. She had too much else going on with the new school year rapidly approaching and the wedding still to deal with. Especially with the saboteur on the loose and the man in question being her main suspect.

A loud, angry buzzing drew Haley from her thoughts and had her on her feet in a second, while the rest of the wedding party conversation was overtaken by a flurry of screams and swatting.

"Bee!" Kendra yelled, whipping her head around to locate the offending insect. "I'm allergic to bees!"

Jared was on his feet in a flash. He pulled his soon-to-be-wife up from the blanket, wrapped her tight in a towel, and pulled her against his chest protectively while the rest of their party searched for the insect.

The bee, however, had landed happily on Mike's empty sandwich bag and was currently interested in the swipes of sticky yellow liquid left behind.

Honey.

"Didn't you know that bees are attracted to honey?" Haley pointed at his sandwich, her tone accusing. She was mostly mad at herself for not realizing the sandwich might attract bees.

"No." Mike gave her an affronted look. "Look, the bee's not hurting anybody. No need to worry. They're important for the environment and decreasing in numbers, you know."

"I don't care what they are. My sister's allergic. She could die if she gets stung. It's completely irresponsible of you to bring food around her that attracts bees." Haley realized she was getting hysterical. "Why would you do that?"

"First of all, calm down." Mike stood and carefully looked over the baggie and cooler to make sure there were no more bees. "Second of all, I had no idea about Kendra's allergy." He leaned to peer past Haley to see her sister. "Sorry."

"No harm done," Kendra said. "It's not something I go around telling people in normal conversation. Hi, I'm Kendra, and bees can kill me."

Haley rolled her eyes, her hands on her hips, still focused on Mike, clinging to her anger even though she realized it was mostly directed at herself. "You should be more careful next time."

"And you should stop overreacting." Mike stepped closer, and Haley took a step back, fumbling over the sand and catching her balance by grasping the edge of one of the umbrellas.

Movement from the periphery of the beach caught

her attention, and she glanced up to the top of the cliff to see a glimpse of jet-black hair. The gardener Emery, looking as unapproachable as she had earlier when they'd arrived at the inn. She had something in her hand but turned away quickly as soon as she saw Haley looking up at her. Weird.

Confused, Haley turned back to Mike, only to find him busy cleaning up the mess from their lunch, including the baggies from their sandwiches and chips. He carefully picked up the baggie with the bee still on it as well and carried them across the beach to a trash bin far from Kendra, where he laid it gently on top of the refuse, not disturbing the bee in the slightest. It was both incredibly endearing and irritating as heck. Okay, she'd admit that he *might* be innocent enough about the whole honey incident, but her suspicions about him were still on high alert.

CHAPTER FIVE

*L*ater that afternoon, Haley was back at the inn, scrubbing sand and sea salt off her skin and mulling over the whole beach incident again. Okay, Mike had seemed as surprised as everyone else about Kendra's allergy revelation, *and* he'd quickly gotten rid of the offending sandwich—humanely too, her not-so-helpful brain pointed out.

As she shampooed and rinsed her hair, she had to give the man begrudging credit. He'd saved an endangered species, calmed things down, and still somehow managed to appear dashing and debonair as he'd saved the day. It was enough to give a girl a serious case of the warm fuzzies, despite those godawful neon palm-tree board shorts the guy had worn.

Trouble was, Haley wasn't just some girl. She was

the maid of honor in her beloved sister's wedding, and she had a duty to make sure things went off perfectly for Kendra. And that included being suspicious of the groom's best man if she had reason.

And so what if the more she saw Mike interacting with Jared and Kendra and the rest of the wedding party, the greater her doubts grew that he would be the one to sabotage the ceremony? If he'd wanted to create chaos today, what better way to do it than with flying, stinging insects. He'd said he hadn't known about Kendra's life-threatening allergy, but if he'd hung out with them for any amount of time, he might have heard about it even if just in passing. And wasn't a honey-and-peanut-butter sandwich just the perfect way to draw bees in droves? Then again, he hadn't been the only one eating them. It looked like Rachel had had one too. Did she eat it because it was Mike's favorite? She'd be the type to try to make a flirty connection with someone that way.

After rinsing the conditioner from her hair, Haley shut off the shower and got out to dry off, the knot of tension in her stomach still tight. Her baby sister could've died on the beach today. Even with her EpiPen. If there'd been a delay in administering the medication or if more than one bee had stung Kendra at a time, the results could've been disastrous. Her sister made jokes about it, but it was deathly serious.

She shuddered as she walked out of the bathroom and pulled on clean clothes—white shorts, a cute navy-and-white-striped top, and matching white sandals. As she combed her wet hair back into a low, slick ponytail, her mind continued to whirl.

Lost sunglasses and busted zippers were one thing, but this incident could have been serious. Maybe the person didn't realize how serious it could have been, or maybe the bee incident was a coincidence, but there was no doubt in Haley's mind—now it was even more important than ever that she find out who was pulling all these little stunts around the inn and put a stop to them. As she fastened her earrings and watch into place, Haley looked out the window and spotted Rachel and one of the groomsmen—Todd—walking in the gardens.

Todd looked politely bored as Rachel continued to flirt outrageously with him. Haley caught snippets of their conversation drifting up to the second floor, names of other members of the wedding party and most likely more gossip. Feeling a tad nosy, Haley decided to head downstairs to see if she could pick up more clues about who was who and who might want to ruin the wedding, but halfway down the stairs, she was confronted by a muscled wall clad in white cotton.

"Hey," Mike said, reaching out a hand to steady Haley as she nearly barreled face-first into him. Zings of awareness shimmered through her bloodstream from the contact before she shrugged off his touch. "Where are you going in such a hurry?"

Heat prickling up her cheeks, she stared up at him and cleared her throat. "Nowhere. Why? Are you following me?"

"Uh, no. We're heading in opposite directions, in case you hadn't noticed." He narrowed his gaze and stepped down a few steps, putting them face-to-face, his arms crossed, as if he harbored some suspicions of his own where she was concerned. "Why don't you like Jared? The truth."

"What? Don't be ridiculous." She looked away fast. "I like him fine. I just don't know him that well, other than his reputation, like I said earlier."

"Right." His tone sounded unconvinced. From where she stood, Haley could see the damp curls at the nape of his neck from his recent shower and smell the clean scent of soap on his skin. "Well, Jared's a good man. Honorable too. I owe him more than I can ever repay."

The admiration and sincerity in his deep voice told Haley he was telling the truth. Mike cared about his friend, maybe even as much as she cared for Kendra. The thought of him, a big muscled guy with a tough exterior, having such a soft heart, had tiny fissures in her well-fortified armor cracking open even more. She shrugged and stepped to the side, putting some much-needed distance between them. "Good to know."

They stared at each other, silent, for several seconds until it became downright uncomfortable. Finally, Haley couldn't take it anymore. "Fine. I do have some reservations about Jared. Mainly because of the things I've heard about him. Some of the same things I've heard about you too." She raised a brow. "I was told you both liked to play the field in your younger days and that you had a new woman every week. I just don't want to see my sister get hurt, that's all."

"Those days were over a long time ago." Mike shook his head and frowned. "The past is the past, and you need to let it go. Jared had some issues after he got out of the military. We both did. But he's better now."

"What kind of issues?"

Mike took a deep breath then exhaled slowly. "They're not important now. What is important is he's very much in love with Kendra and totally committed to their future together."

"What about your discharge? Is that why you owe him?"

"We don't like to talk about that anymore."

"Why not? Was it that bad?"

"Yeah, actually, it was." The warmth in his blue eyes

froze over, and his broad shoulders slumped. Haley couldn't help feeling a pang of sympathy and remorse toward the guy. She'd overstepped a line, obviously, but there was no way to take back her questions now, no matter how much she might want to.

"Look, suffice it to say he saved my life. Literally. And got in trouble because of it." He shuffled his feet and stared at anything but her, clearly uncomfortable discussing the incident. Still, there had to be something he wasn't telling her. People didn't get other-than-honorable-conditions-discharges for saving someone's life. They got medals.

"But—" she started, before he raised his hand, cutting her off.

"It's not what you think, okay? Not everything is as it appears." Mike continued up the stairs, leaving her to stare after him.

As she headed down to the first floor, she muttered to herself, "I don't care how things *appear*. No one is going to mess up my sister's wedding. No one."

Back in his room, Mike stretched out on his bed and stared up at the ceiling, the events of the day replaying in his head and a certain prim redhead foremost in his thoughts. Haley had all but called him a playboy just now, but that was laughable. His playboy days were long gone.

Besides, who'd want me now, with my scars?

A knock at the door sounded, jarring him out of his pity party.

"Come in."

Jared entered and took a seat in the chair across from the bed. "Saw Haley in the hall. Was she up here with you? Maybe getting to know you better?"

Mike rolled his eyes as his buddy waggled his brows. "Nah. She's so prickly it'd be like hugging a porcupine, man. All she's concerned about is somebody trying to sabotage your wedding."

"What?"

Mike filled him in on all the little mishaps that had happened so far and his own concerns about who might be causing them.

"I don't know, man. Sounds like just a bunch of random stuff," Jared said, scrubbing a hand over his face. "But after that scare with the bee at the beach, got to admit maybe you have a point." He sat back and sighed. "Kendra could've died. If someone is doing this even for a joke or something, they crossed a line."

"Hey." Mike sat up and gave his friend his best serious look. "That's why I won't back down until I catch the guilty party. I'm your best man, okay? It's my job to make sure everything is safe and secure for your big day. I won't let anything happen to Kendra or to you. I promise. No way will anyone mess up your future together." He threw his legs over the side of the mattress, then frowned. "I wonder why Haley was in such a hurry to get downstairs though? She nearly barreled right over the top of me."

"Did you ask her?"

"I did, but she never answered me. Then she started asking me a lot of questions about our military days and our past, like *she* was suspicious of *me*." His frown deepened. "But she's the one who's been around when all these wonky things happened. She knows her sister's allergic to bee stings too."

"Come on, man. No way would Haley harm *Kendra*. She loves her too much. If she wants to stop the wedding, she'd harm *me*."

"Maybe. But I'm going to keep an eye on her anyway, just in case."

"Right." Jared chuckled and stretched out his long legs. "You sure that's the real reason you want to follow her around, buddy?"

Mike gave a one-shoulder shrug and grinned. "She *is* cute. Watching her won't be a hardship."

"Yeah. Connor family trait. All the girls are pretty."

"That they are." Mike stood. "Want to go downstairs for a snack? I'm starving again."

"Sure." Jared followed Mike out of the room. They stopped in the kitchen and enjoyed a few homemade chocolate chip cookies fresh from the oven then walked outside to find the rest of the guys and see what else there was to do around the inn.

As they passed the open conservatory doors, Mike spotted Ginny standing inside. "Hey. We were just wondering what's to do this afternoon."

"Oh, well, I think some of the bridesmaids were playing bocce ball on the side lawn near the meadow," she said. "Go around the corner ahead and you should see them."

"Great, thanks." He trailed behind Jared, both happy and annoyed to find Haley and Kendra playing the game. Looked like he'd have to add round two of battle with Haley to his afternoon schedule.

CHAPTER SIX

*G*inny was glad for the sunny weather to keep her guests occupied with outdoor activities. She was also glad all the sports equipment and games she'd pulled out of the old toolshed in the back were being used. Once this wedding was over, she really needed to see about having it replaced with a newer, bigger model. With having Emery here now and all of her equipment, they needed more space. And honestly, it was an eyesore in its current condition, with peeling paint and slanting walls. Not to mention a fire hazard. She was lucky the local inspector hadn't written her up during his last visit to the inn. Then again, she had a sneaking suspicion the older man was sweet on Maisie, her cook, and a good helping of homemade pie never hurt anyone.

Ah, well. She'd call a handyman to tear it down as soon as she got this wedding finished and her current guests departed. Right now, she had bigger concerns. Namely, all the freak little accidents happening around the place.

"Have you seen anything strange around here lately?" Ginny asked, turning to Maisie, who was stirring a huge ceramic bowl of batter. Hard to believe the gray-haired, grandmotherly-type woman wasn't much older than Ginny.

"You mean like those salt shakers moving around?" Maisie asked with a grin.

"No. Not like that." Ginny laughed it off. "Things to do with the wedding or some of the guests acting oddly."

"No, ma'am. I'll keep my eye out though."

"Thank you." Ginny didn't like to admit it, but she was worried. She'd noticed a few odd things lately. Well, odder than usual anyway.

Some of the white taper candles she'd scattered about the inn, per Haley's instructions, had been found broken or bent at odd angles as if partially melted. Then there were the pink heart decorations for the reception she'd laid out in the library for storage until they were ready to hang. This morning she'd found them smudged with what looked like dirt. She shook her head, perplexed. Why would anyone want to disrupt what should be the happiest day of Jared's and Kendra's lives when they were so obviously in love?

"Maybe it's your ghost, Dooley, messing about again," Maisie said.

"Maybe." But Dooley had told Ginny he'd *help* her with the inn, not hurt her business. If she even believed a ghost had actually talked to her, that was. Then again, lots of good things had happened since that encounter with Dooley. Her rooms were booked through the autumn, she had all the major renovations done on the place, and she'd managed to find and maintain a full staff around the inn, including her new gardener.

As if on cue, Emery came in from the mudroom, her shirt still streaked with mud from the gardens, but her hands and face were scrubbed clean. Her dark hair gleamed nearly blue in the sunlight, and her olive skin glowed with health and vitality.

"Speak of the devil." Maisie waved the girl over to get one of her famous peanut butter cookies from the tray fresh out of the oven. "You do fantastic work with those plants, Emery girl, but you're far too quiet. You need to speak up around here so we know you're coming."

EMERY SANTOS TOOK a couple huge cookies then sat at the kitchen table to eat. Both Maisie and Ginny had been really nice to her since she'd moved to Boulder Point, but she cautioned herself not to get too close. Chances were high she wouldn't be staying long, and small towns had a way of prying into a person's past. That was something she could not risk.

"How are you settling in?" Ginny asked, taking a seat across from Emery at the table. "The gardens are looking magnificent. I tried to help you out earlier on that patch along the side of the house, but you do a far better job than me."

Emery smiled briefly then took another bite of cookie. From the moment she'd interviewed for the maintenance position here at the inn, she'd known Ginny was a sweet lady—and also a little sad. In fact, she reminded Emery of her own mother. All the more reason to keep her distance. She got the impression Ginny liked to keep people a bit at bay too, with the way she was always politely cool around everyone—friendly but not personal. Though it was hard to imagine Ginny's reasons for wanting her privacy were the same as Emery's.

"You keep doing such a fabulous job with the landscaping around here and I'm sensing a raise in your future, young lady." Ginny gave her a warm smile. Pride swelled inside Emery. She always tried to do her best, no matter what the circumstances. "Do you have any ideas for the gardens, maybe things I've not planted you think would be good additions?"

"Well," Emery said after swallowing another bite of cookie. "You've got lots of roses and spring- and summer-blooming plants, but I'd like to add some mums and maybe some black-eyed Susans, so there'll be color into the fall. With your bookings extending so late into the year, the guests would enjoy them."

"Oh, that's a great idea." Maisie set a plate of leftover peanut butter cookies on the table in front of Emery. The others were done up fancy on trays for the guests outside. They were having some kind of tea party thing for the bridesmaids in the conservatory later, if Emery remembered right. She tried to stay out of the way of the guests as much as possible. Too many people around made her nervous. Besides, she was hardly fancy party material these days.

She'd had a close call earlier, when she'd wanted to go down to the beach for a few minutes after checking on the hives at the edge of the property. Technically, she wasn't supposed to go down there when guests were present, but she'd thought they'd all been inside the inn, and the urge to dip her toes in the ocean had been almost undeniable. But once she'd seen them all down there, she turned and rushed back to the safety and seclusion of her gardens.

"I saw Angus's still around," Emery said, snatching another cookie from the plate. She hadn't been eating well the past few months, what with all the running and hiding, so these warm, delicious cookies were like manna from heaven.

"Angus?" Ginny frowned. "Who's that?"

"That orange-striped tabby in the back gardens." Emery shrugged. "He's kind of red colored, so I call him Angus. Seems like someone named Angus would have red hair."

"Oh." Ginny gave her a small smile. "Right. He does seem to like all the sun back there on the patio. Though I was hoping he'd find another home soon. He's not mine."

"You feed him though. I've seen the bowls of food and water. That makes you a good person, Mrs. Flynn. Not many take the time these days to concern themselves with those less fortunate."

"Well, I don't want the poor thing to starve. Looks like he's been through enough already. We all have." Ginny looked away, staring out the window as a shadow of grief passed over her face. There then gone, so fast Emery would've missed it if she hadn't been paying attention. Seemed Emery wasn't the only one hiding her feelings. Ginny sighed then turned back, her polite smile firmly in place once more. "You haven't seen anything odd around the inn lately, have you?"

Emery stopped mid-bite of cookie and did her best to hide her wariness. She set her food down and cleared her throat, wiping her hands on the front of her cargo shorts. "What do you mean by odd?"

"You know, guests snooping around where they shouldn't be, maybe someone tampering with the decorations or inn property, anything like that."

"Oh." Emery stared at her hands clasped in her lap. Truth was, she *had* seen some odd things. No one really paid much attention to the gardener, so she was privy to all sorts of private moments as she worked behind the thick shrubs and vegetation surrounding the inn. Things most people would not want seen or heard. Then there'd been that whole bee kerfuffle down at the beach. Not that she'd mention that to Mrs. Flynn. Part of her job was building up the bee colony in the old hives, and while Emery might not be staying in Boulder Point long, while she was here, she needed this job. "No, ma'am."

"Well, if you do see something, will you please let me know?"

Emery nodded then continued to eat her cookie as Ginny stood and left the room. Through the screen door, trills of feminine laughter floated through the air, and

Emery's heart pinched. Those sisters in the wedding made her homesick for her own family...

She quickly shook off those bittersweet thoughts and shoved the rest of her last cookie into her mouth. No time to think about her family now. Time to get back to work. Emery pushed to her feet and headed for the door.

"Thank you again for the cookies," she said to Maisie over her shoulder as she pushed outside again into the summer sunshine.

CHAPTER SEVEN

*H*aley spent the rest of the afternoon observing the wedding party playing bocce ball and relaxing on the back porch. Everyone seemed happy and carefree and got along fine. Had she been imagining that someone wanted to ruin the wedding? No one acted suspicious at all. It was enough to drive a maid of honor nuts. Even hours later, as they finished the huge cookout on the side yard of the inn, she couldn't quite figure out if someone was really trying to ruin Kendra's big day.

"Hey, do you think Jared's acting a bit strange tonight?" Rachel asked, leaning closer to Haley at the long picnic table, the gingham tablecloth ruffling in the breeze. Somehow, they'd ended up seated beside each other, though not by Haley's choice.

"Maybe he's just nervous," Haley said, shrugging. "Grooms get cold feet sometimes."

"Maybe." Rachel moved closer, whispering, "But I just saw him take Simone into the meadow. It's getting dark and that area is pretty secluded, you know, if you didn't want anyone to see you disappear."

"What exactly are you implying?" Haley snapped, sudden anger rising within her on her sister's behalf. "You think Jared's fooling around?"

"No." Rachel shushed her. "And keep your voice down. I don't think he's like that anymore. Besides, Jared's head over heels for Kendra, don't worry. Trust me. I've known him a long time, and I'd be able to tell if he wasn't. He wouldn't cheat on her."

"So why would he take another woman into that field?"

"No idea." Rachel flashed a sticky-sweet smile then got up and walked away, leaving Haley to stew.

No matter how Kendra and Mike gushed about him, deep down Haley still didn't trust Jared, no matter how sweet and nice and attentive he was around her sister. Maybe she was being overly critical, but Haley was taking on the role of the father Kendra didn't have. Wouldn't a dad be overly critical of the guy his daughter wanted to marry?

Jared might be handsome and a successful doctor-to-be, but he of all people should've known better than to allow Kendra anywhere near that bee on the beach. Why hadn't he rushed her away? He knew the risks, knew it could've killed her, and sure he did wrap her in the towel, but still, he stayed near the group where the bee was.

Maybe that's why he didn't freak out when it happened. Maybe that's what he wanted. To have Kendra incapacitated on the day of the ceremony so she couldn't go through with their vows. Rachel had said he was acting weird and nervous. Maybe it was more than cold feet. Maybe he wanted to call the whole thing off. Resolute, Haley stood and headed for the meadow behind the inn.

If Jared was up to no good, she was going to find out about it.

She never made it past the edge of the yard, however, before Kendra ran up to her. "Where are you going, sis?"

"Just taking a walk in the meadow," Haley said, hoping her lie sounded believable. "Work off some of that pulled pork from dinner."

"Great, I'll come with you."

"Oh, no. You don't want to do that." Haley fumbled her words, feeling like an idiot. The last thing she wanted was for Kendra to follow her and catch Jared cheating. If he was, then Haley would find a way to break it to her gently. "Look, they're starting a bonfire, and you always love those. Why don't you go get some s'mores started?"

Kendra narrowed her gaze and placed her hands on her hips. "If I didn't know better, I'd think you were trying to get rid of me."

"Get rid of you?" Haley's snort of laughter sounded fake even to her own ears. "Don't be—"

"Don't be what?" Mike walked out of the tall grass nearby, a mason jar in his hands. Almost a dozen fireflies glowed inside. When he saw the frown on her face, he glanced at the jar. "We're going to let them go, don't worry."

"Oh!" Kendra clapped her hands like a little kid. "I want a jar. I'll bring you one too, Haley. Be right back."

She took off, leaving Haley and Mike alone again. Awkwardness curdled between them, and Haley shifted her weight to her other foot, staring off into the distance, looking anywhere but at him. She could make out the shapes of members of the wedding party scattered across the landscape, some running after fireflies, some standing and talking. All smiling and laughing and generally having a good time.

"So, you have a problem with me catching bugs too?" Mike said finally, a hint of amusement in his tone.

"What?" Haley glanced sideways at him, doing her best not to notice he looked more carefree tonight. Laid back was a good look on him. Not that he had a bad look. Or that she'd noticed. "No. I don't care what you do with your bugs."

His lips twitched into a full-blown smile, and there was no mistaking his humor now. Even his blue eyes sparkled with suppressed mirth.

"Well, technically, they aren't *my* bugs." Mike held up his jar to eye level. Inside, the fireflies flitted around, their glowing behinds shining into the gathering twilight. "If anything, I'd say they were the property of the inn. Though I can't really see any tiny logos branded on their tummies. So maybe they're free-range bugs."

"Very funny." Haley placed her hands on her hips and tapped the toe of her flip-flop on the grass. Honestly, she didn't know why Mike got under her skin so badly. Under different circumstances, she would've liked the guy. He really was smart and funny and polite to a fault. He was even her type—tall, blond, tanned, and toned with muscle. But the fact he was here, at her sister's wedding, and perhaps trying to sabotage the whole thing just ticked her off.

That's what she was telling herself, anyway.

"Here you go," Kendra said, running back up to hand Haley an empty container. "I'm going to head across the field to where Jared and the other guys are. You kids have fun."

Haley watched her sister run through the tall grass like some heroine out of a sappy romance novel. They were so in love it made Haley's heart pinch. Heck, even Rachel seemed to have hooked up with one of the groomsmen and was laughing and joking around with him.

Feeling a bit lonely and deflated, Haley glanced back at Mike, only to find him still watching her, his gaze far too perceptive for her comfort. "What?"

"Nothing," he said, shaking his head and looking away. "Just wondered why you do that to yourself."

"Do what?"

"Close yourself off like that." He shrugged. "Not that it's any of my business."

"That's right. It's not." She unscrewed the lid from her Mason jar then took off in the opposite direction of the others across the field. "Now, if you'll excuse me."

He didn't excuse her, apparently. Instead, he followed her into the tall grass. "There you go again. Running away."

"I am not running anywhere. I'm trying to catch these stupid bugs." She swiped her jar through the air and came up empty. "Go away. You're scaring them away."

"If anyone's scaring them, it's you." Mike stood beside

her to explain proper firefly-catching technique. "See, you don't swoop about willy-nilly. You wait, patiently, for them to pass close enough, then you gently scoop the jar over them. They don't even realize they've been caught. And don't forget to put the lid on tight, or they'll sneak out."

Haley rolled her eyes and kept walking. Truth was, she didn't want to catch any bugs anyway. But she felt like she had to participate, for Kendra's sake. And no way would she trap Jared doing anything untoward now, with Kendra close by. She and Mike walked along in silence, with her thinking and him catching more bugs, until his jar glowed bright like a veritable firefly lantern. They stopped near the cliff's edge and stared out across the ocean.

"Find any more tampered-with decorations?" Mike asked out of the blue, his voice quiet above the steady crash of the ocean waves below.

"No. Not yet." Haley crossed her arms. Was he asking because he wanted to know if she'd discovered his latest sabotage, or did he really want to help?

The cool breeze was stronger here and chilled her slightly sunburnt skin. She should've used more sunscreen on the beach earlier. Speaking of the beach... "I think that bee attack was more than enough for one day."

Mike snorted. "Bee attack. You do have a flair for the dramatic, don't you?"

"Do not."

"It was one bee, and I got rid of it without any harm done."

"Glad you're so cavalier with my sister's life. There could've been a lot of harm done if she'd gotten stung."

He sighed. "Is it possible that you're overreacting? That the bee was just a fluke?"

The tiredness in his tone was echoed by the slight sag in his big, broad shoulders.

Haley hung her head. She was tired too. It had been a long day in an already long week. Maybe Mike was right. Maybe they could call a truce for tonight. "Sorry. I'm just worried about my sister and the wedding, that's all."

"I know." He looked over at her with a small smile. "I'm worried for Jared too. He's my best bud. I want his special day to be perfect."

"Exactly." They stood side by side and stared out over the sea, stars twinkling above and the heat of him penetrating through Haley's thin, striped shirt offsetting the cold. She tamped down the urge to snuggle closer to his side and rubbed her arms. "Well, we should probably get back to the others."

"Can I ask you something?"

His low voice brushed over her like crushed velvet, and she shivered. "Sure."

"Are you jealous of your sister? Of what she and Jared have?"

"No." Haley frowned. "Why would you ask me that? I love my sister, more than life itself."

"You do a lot for her, don't you?" Mike faced her, his blue eyes dark as midnight in the moonlight, his expression kind. "But I have to wonder sometimes, as I watch you cater to her every whim. When do you take time for yourself? Who caters to you, Haley?"

Her chest squeezed tight with the truth of his words. She did do a lot for Kendra, perhaps more than she should, but she owed her. Haley owed Kendra, owed her a stable home and a happy childhood and all the things they'd never had because their parents had been taken from them far too soon. It was a burden she willingly carried. Kendra's happiness meant everything to her. Her own didn't matter. As long as Kendra had what she needed, things were all good.

"It doesn't matter." Haley started back across the field, only to have Mike take her elbow, stopping her.

"But what if it does, Haley?" His soft tone made goose bumps of awareness stand up on her skin. Why did he have to be so nice to her tonight? Why couldn't he have kept on being the womanizing jerk she'd expected him to be? The rough pad of his thumb stroked the sensitive skin on the inside of her arm, and she bit her lip. It had been a long time since someone had touched her like that. "Tell me why you feel responsible for your sister. Tell me why you don't think you're important too."

She opened her mouth, ready to spill all her secrets, crazy as that sounded. They barely knew each other. Haley never told anyone about her guilt over killing their parents, yet here she was ready to tell Mike, a guy with the kindest blue eyes she'd ever seen and horrible scars of his own.

"Haley? Where are you?" Kendra's voice called out across the field. "We're ready to set the fireflies free."

The disruption was enough to break the spell between her and Mike, though a lingering intimacy still buzzed between them. Haley stepped back from him and swallowed hard. "Guess we should get back to the others."

"Guess so."

They walked silently across the meadow, the tall grass swishing around them, until they reached the edge of the inn yard again. The others were gathered around one of the picnic tables while Kendra held court over her wedding party.

"There you are, sis," Kendra said, leaning past Jared

to see Haley. "C'mon over here and open your jar. For each bug that escapes, you get to make a wish."

Haley and Mike joined the small crowd, and she watched as the wedding party opened their jars and let the bugs out, each person closing their eyes and whispering silent wishes.

By the time it got around to Haley, she went to open her jar, her stomach swooping when she realized she hadn't secured the lid properly. It had fallen off, and the jar was empty. Before she could panic, however, Mike thrust his full jar into her hands and took her empty one for himself.

He held up the hollow Mason jar and shrugged. "No luck for me tonight."

"But," Haley started, looking at Mike. "These are your wishes."

"You make them for both of us," he said under his breath, giving her a quick wink. "I'm sure you're better at that than me."

"Go on, sis," Kendra said, holding Jared's hand. "Make them for something good. You never know when you'll get to make another wish!"

All eyes turned to her, and Haley's cheeks prickled with heat. She unscrewed the lid on Mike's jar, and fireflies flew out one by one, their tiny lights flickering in the night sky.

Mike leaned in and whispered. "Go on. Make us a wish."

Haley lowered her head and squeezed her eyes closed, knowing deep in her heart exactly what she wanted. A whirlwind, lasting, precious romance just like Jared and Kendra's. She was tired of being alone, tired of having no one to care about her needs, her wants, her future. Beside her, Mike's arm brushed hers, and more tingles of warmth shimmered through her nerve endings.

MIKE STUDIED Haley's downturned face, her expression thoughtful as she made her wishes. He still wasn't quite sure what had possessed him to give her his jar of fire-flies, but seeing how happy she was now, he was glad he had.

Besides, he'd given up on believing in wishes a long time ago.

She'd been so close to telling him something back there in that field, something he sensed she didn't share with many people. And now he was more intrigued by her than ever. Suddenly his earlier thoughts about Haley being the one that was causing all the incidents sounded ridiculous. She didn't seem like the type, and he doubted she would do that to her sister. She was too devoted.

Which meant that either it was someone else, or all the incidents had simply been a coincidence.

Probably coincidence. Nothing major had happened. The bee incident could have been a big deal, but it was one little bee, and bees were known to be outdoors in summer. Plus, he'd seen beehives at the edge of the field. Had he known about Kendra's allergy, he never would have eaten a sandwich with honey even if Rachel and Simone had been nice enough to make his favorite.

Mike couldn't imagine that anyone in the wedding party would want to put a damper on Kendra and Jared's big day, so all those little incidents were just some kind of fluke. That was good, because he didn't want to suspect Haley. As best man and maid of honor, they needed to work together to make sure Kendra and Jared's day was extra special, and he had some ideas he wanted to fly by her for the rehearsal dinner and the wedding reception. Plus he was surprised to discover that he wanted to get to know her better as a person, as a friend, and possibly as a woman too.

That last one concerned him the most. He had no business thinking about Kendra's sister as anything other than a bossy pest at his best bud's wedding. Remembering the pain of Courtney's betrayal, Mike realized that Haley could never be anything more than a fleeting acquaintance. When the wedding was over, they would go their separate ways. Probably never see each other again. Yet she was like a puzzle that he couldn't resist trying to figure out even if he knew she could never be anything more.

Then their arms brushed, and something deep in his chest twitched to life, something he'd thought long dead and buried, something he'd imagined had burned up and turned to ash from the same fire that had scarred his body.

His heart.

CHAPTER EIGHT

*G*inny woke up the following morning to find Donald's photo turned away from her again on the nightstand. How did that keep happening? She always had it facing her so that she could see Donald's smile first thing in the morning, but a few times she'd awakened to find it facing away from her.

Her thoughts immediately turned to Dooley, then she laughed at herself. It was silly to think a ghost would move a picture. She rolled over and rubbed her eyes, saying sleepily, "I've kept those shakers where they are. I thought we had a deal and you were going to help."

Great, now she was talking to ghosts. Maybe she was becoming a bit too standoffish in her relationships.

After getting ready for the day, Ginny headed downstairs to the kitchen, her mind a bit stressed over the upcoming events. The big rehearsal dinner for the wedding was that night, and even though the food was being catered by Reid Callahan, Stacy's fiancé, there was still a lot to get done—the table settings, the decorations, going over the seating charts one more time.

Some of her tension must've shown, because as soon as Ginny took a seat at the table, Maisie was there with a hot mug of tea and a kind smile. "Not my place to say, ma'am, but you need to stop fretting. If you have concerns about the dinner, say something to Stacy. That's her job, after all."

"I know, I know." Ginny stirred some honey into her chamomile. "And it's not the dinner I'm worried about so much. I'm sure Stacy will handle it all well. It's just hard to turn off my internal mother hen sometimes. Especially when it's so important that things be perfect."

"I know, ma'am." Maisie patted her shoulder. "But we're all here for you. Don't be afraid to lean on us for help once in a while. Now what can I get you for breakfast today?"

After nibbling on some dry toast and finishing her tea, Ginny did her usual morning walk-through of the inn to make sure things were in order for her guests for the day, then headed out onto the back patio to enjoy the beauty of the sunrise over the Atlantic. She was always up before the dawn, an old habit from the days when she and Donald used to run their hotels together. Now getting up before everyone else was more important than ever.

She leaned against the wrought iron railing and inhaled the fresh, salty sea air, the briny tang of fish stinging her nose and bringing her senses alive. She really did love it here. Maine brought something new to life in her soul, made her ready to get back out and experience the world again.

Movement in the rosebushes made her swivel fast, her pulse kicking up a notch.

In the golden-pink rays of early sunshine, she spotted the orange tabby, Angus, munching on kibble from the bowl she'd put out a few days prior. Emery stood a few yards away, trimmers in hand. The cat she wasn't surprised to see. The gardener? She was.

Seemed Ginny wasn't the only person who liked to get an early start in the morning. Frankly, she'd not paid much attention to Emery's comings and goings since she'd started working at the inn. As long as her staff got their work done and maintained her high standards, that was enough for Ginny. But now seeing Emery working alone in the gardens so early in the morning made her wonder even more about the secretive girl.

"Good morning." Ginny forced a smile, trying to

hide the fact she had been startled. "Didn't expect to see you up and about yet, Emery."

The girl glanced down at the cat, who was now twining itself around her ankles, then reached down to pet it. "Morning, Mrs. Flynn. I wanted to get a head start on the day's work so I don't interrupt the guests."

"Makes sense." Ginny chuckled as Angus purred loudly under Emery's attention. Then the cat turned to Ginny, as if expecting the same treatment from her, and her smile faltered. She stepped aside and waved her hand in the air. "Okay, shoo now, little kitty. I can't get attached to you. Go."

Angus meowed then darted back into the thick foliage again.

"Odd. That's the most I've seen of him in a while." She glanced back at Emery again. "Usually he stays hidden in the bushes whenever anyone's out here on the patio."

"Why hadn't you named him before?" Emery asked, her head tilted and her dark eyes watchful. "Unless you like Angus, of course."

"Angus's fine, I suppose. But I told you, he's not mine. Why would I name him?" Ginny shrugged and turned to face the ocean again. She didn't want to know the cat's name or that it was a boy or that it liked to get scratched behind his ears. All of that only led to attachment, and attachment led to heartbreak. "Besides, next thing he'll be wanting to come inside the inn, and I can't have that. Some guests are allergic."

"Hmm." Emery didn't sound entirely convinced by Ginny's explanation, but she went back to trimming the hedges just the same. "Well, these Northern bush honeysuckles are sure blooming up a storm."

As she snipped away at a few errant branches, the sweet smell of the flowers filled the air and got Ginny to thinking about the evening's event again. "Maybe we can add some to the centerpieces tonight. Some of these roses too."

"That's a good idea, Mrs. Flynn." Emery didn't look up from her work. "Clipping the flowers from the rosebushes will help them bloom well into the fall. I'll get started on them as soon as I finish with these hedges."

"Great. Thank you." A seagull squawked overhead, probably looking for its morning meal. Ginny looked up at it, then back to where Emery had been standing just moments before, only to find the girl gone without a sound. Ginny chuckled and shook her head as she headed back inside the inn to find Stacy.

Seemed Emery was as mysterious as her ghost and could disappear just as quickly.

CHAPTER NINE

*H*aley got up that morning feeling nearly as tired as when she'd gone to bed the night before. Not that her body hadn't been worn out. Spending all that time outside, chasing after whirlwind Kendra, would do that to a gal. But her mind hadn't cooperated. Instead, she'd spent the whole night tossing and turning with thoughts of a certain blond-haired, blue-eyed best man swirling through her brain.

She brushed her teeth and took a shower, pulled on clothes she hoped matched, then headed downstairs to find some caffeine. It was only seven forty-five, but the rest of the wedding party was already in the dining room, gorging themselves on the all-you-could-eat breakfast buffet and chattering loudly about the upcoming rehearsal dinner.

Dragging herself over to the coffee cart, Haley fixed herself a mug of strong black coffee then pondered the food selections for the morning. Scrambled eggs with cheese, home-fried potatoes, crispy bacon, sausage gravy, and buttermilk biscuits. On another long table was an assortment of fresh fruit, rolls, cold cereal, and juices. She settled on some bacon, a bowl of ripe Maine blueberries, and a whole-wheat bagel with peanut butter then carried her plate to an empty table by the window and settled in to await the return of her energy.

"This seat taken?" She looked up to see Mike's smiling face, a fresh wave of awareness rippling through her.

Channeling all her effort to keep her expression flat, Haley waved her hand at the empty chair. "No."

"Thanks." He plopped down, seemingly undeterred by her lack of enthusiasm. "I wanted to talk to you about the rehearsal dinner tonight while I had a chance. As best man and maid of honor, it's our duty to say a few words about our beloved friend and sister before the wedding. Maybe offer them some life advice."

Haley nibbled on her bagel, staring down into her coffee instead of at him. She still wasn't sure what it was about Mike that affected her so much, but every time he was close to her, it was as if all of her senses kicked into overdrive, getting her all flustered and confused. Especially now. Even though she wasn't looking at him, she could feel the heat of his legs close to hers under the table, could smell his shampoo and the citrusy scent of his aftershave. Could even hear the smile in his voice and his affection for the newlyweds. It was enough to drive a girl crazy.

"I doubt the happy couple would appreciate any words of wisdom I might have about their relationship." She met his gaze at last, her lack of sleep making her snippy. "And Kendra hates it when I tell all my sappy stories about the two of us growing up."

Mike's sunny smile dipped into a frown. "Don't tell me you still have your doubts about Jared. I'd think after saving Kendra's life down on the beach yesterday, he'd pretty much proved his loyalty."

"Saving her life?" Haley snorted then noticed the other people in the room glancing their way and lowered her voice. "In case you didn't notice, I'm the one who alerted everyone to my sister's allergy, not Jared. And you got rid of the bee, not him."

"Is that what's sticking in your craw then?" Mike sat back and crossed his arms. "The fact you're being replaced?"

"What? Don't be ridiculous." Haley devoured several bites of blueberries and half her bagel, hoping maybe he'd go away. He didn't. "All I've ever wanted was for my sister to be happy and meet the man of her dreams. And if she thinks Jared is the one for her, then I pray she's right."

"But you don't approve."

"Why do you care what I think?"

He exhaled slowly and narrowed his gaze on her, his tone sounding as exasperated as she felt. "I've been asking myself that same question."

"Let me know when you come up with an answer." Honestly, she couldn't quite believe she was being so rude to him. She never acted this way with anyone. She was always the polite one, the responsible one, the one everyone relied on to be perfect. But there was something about Mike Sanderson that set off all her warning bells. He stirred things up inside her—disturbing, wild, brazen things—and she wanted to make him go away. "Don't hurt yourself though, thinking too hard."

To her surprise, he laughed. A deep, rich, full-belly laugh that did all kinds of crazy things to her nervous system. He gave her an indulgent smile and shook his head. "That's why I like you, Haley. You don't take any of my crap."

She watched him over the rim of her mug while she sipped her coffee, grateful the cup hid her smile. "That's the only reason you like me, huh?"

"The only one I'll cop to at the moment."

And now she was flirting with the guy? Holy cow! Her lack of sleep must be affecting her way more than she thought. Haley could count on one hand the number of times she'd flirted with a guy, including this one. Yet there was something about Mike that seemed to bring out her playful side too. Finally, she pushed her empty breakfast plate away and leaned back in her chair. "So, about these speeches."

"Yeah."

"You have yours planned out already?"

"Somewhat," Mike said, smiling at Ginny as she came by to refill their water. "I kind of riffed on what I was planning to say at the reception. About how close Jared and I got in the military, about how we have each other's back no matter what, about how I'll always be here for him and now Kendra too, whatever they may need."

"Wow." Haley set her mug down. "That sounds really touching. I haven't even started on my speech for the reception yet, let alone anything for tonight."

"Are you kidding?" Mike sat forward, resting his muscular forearms on the table. His tanned skin contrasted sharply with the pale yellow of his T-shirt, and tiny golden hairs sparkled against his skin in the sunlight streaming through the windows. Those raised white scars on his left arm and neck caught her eye again, making her wonder exactly what had happened to him and Jared in the Army and exactly how Jared had saved his life. "Took me a month to write mine for the reception. And I've been working on the one for tonight since we got here."

Haley shrugged. "I'm a pretty fast writer. And I prefer to speak a bit more spontaneously, you know. From the heart."

"Hmm." He continued watching her, his gaze wary. "There you go again. Why do you do that?"

"Do what?" She halted with another strip of bacon halfway to her mouth.

"You have this way of saying something polite but at the same time closing the other person out." Mike shook his head, his scowl deepening. "I think you're hiding something."

"Seriously?" Haley rolled her eyes. "And how did you deduce that, Sherlock?"

"Well, let's see. Every time I ask you something about yourself, you close up like a clam. You want to know what I think?"

"Can't wait." Her dull tone suggested the opposite.

"I think you've used your sister as a shield up to this point. I think you've been so busy taking care of her, catering to her every whim, that you're scared to death now to think about life after this wedding. I think you're quaking in your pretty little sandals at the thought of having no one to live for but yourself after this."

Haley exhaled slowly and swallowed her food, though it could've been cardboard for all she tasted it. Much as it galled her to admit, Mike was right. She was terrified of what awaited her after this week. Even though she and Kendra lived miles apart, they talked every day. Sometimes more than once. Would that still happen now that Kendra had Jared to talk to at home?

Somehow going home to her quiet apartment in her quiet Nebraska neighborhood with her few quiet friends and no one on the romance front seemed very lonely. Not that she'd tell him any of that. The guy was already too cocky for his own good. She crossed her arms and arched a brow. "Where'd you get your psychology degree, Shrinks-R-Us?"

"Thanks for proving my point."

Haley narrowed her eyes, ready to retaliate, but before she got the chance, she was interrupted by Kendra and Jared arriving at their table.

"About time you two got to know each other better," Jared said, clapping Mike on the shoulder. "Been telling him you two have more in common than you think. He's a great guy, Haley. Better snap him up before one of these other ladies does."

"Oh no," Haley and Mike said in unison. "It's not like that."

Kendra gave her sister a knowing stare. "It sure looked like that from where I was sitting. Hey, sis. Don't knock love until you try it." She slipped her arm around Jared's waist and snuggled up to his side, kissing him on the cheek. "I just want you to be as happy as we are."

Haley gave them a wan smile, her cheeks heating. A quick glance at Mike showed him in much the same predicament. She would've taken a measure of joy in his discomfort if she hadn't been feeling the same agony herself.

"Well, we're off to do some hiking on the cliffs. Ginny said the views are spectacular, and we wanted to get some shots before everything gets too crazy with the ceremony."

"Right. Sure." Haley nodded. "Have fun. And be careful. And don't forget your EpiPen!"

Kendra waved as she and Jared walked away, totally engrossed in each other.

"Well, that was awkward," Mike said, scrubbing a hand over his face. He looked around at all the other now-deserted tables then back to Haley. "Got plans today?"

She shrugged. "Just hanging around the inn, writing the speech you so helpfully reminded me of."

"Right." He chuckled, the low, deep sound smoothing over her frazzled nerves like velvet, somehow calming them. "Listen, I know we got off on the wrong foot yesterday, but how about we spend the day together. We can go over our speeches, get to know each other better." At her startled look, he held up his hands. "Strictly as friends, promise. Trust me, relationships are definitely not my thing. Not anymore. I do know how to have a good time though. At least I used to. What do you say?"

She wanted to tell him no, tell him she had a headache, and hide out in her room alone all day to brood and contemplate her lonely future. But instead, much to her surprise, she found herself saying, "Okay. Let's do it."

"Great." Mike stood and walked toward the door, his broad smile white against his tanned skin. "Meet you out front on the porch in ten minutes."

"WHAT EXACTLY DO you think this is?" Mike asked, holding up what looked like a small metal medieval knight's helmet, complete with a pointy noseguard. After spending the last two hours going over their respective speeches, he and Haley had wandered into downtown

Boulder Point to do some sightseeing and buy some decorations she wanted to add to the tables at the rehearsal dinner that night. He'd been pleasantly surprised after he'd broken through her initial hard-candy shell this morning to find she'd been good company today. Funny, smart, witty as hell. In fact, he couldn't remember when he'd laughed more with a woman. "It's only four inches tall."

She put her hands on her hips. "Hey now, don't be making fun of the vertically challenged."

Even though Mike knew she was joking, her undertone carried the hurt of years of being made fun of. Mike's heart squeezed, and he put the item down. He knew exactly how that felt.

"I would never do that. Been made fun of quite a bit myself." He self-consciously plucked at the collar of his T-shirt to hide as much of his scar as he could.

Haley's face softened, their eyes met, and Mike saw through the tough exterior to the insecure girl that Haley really was, and in that second he felt a strange bond forming.

She jerked her eyes away and looked back down at the helmet, her voice soft. "I know you wouldn't." She bent closer to inspect the thing. "No idea what it is. Maybe from a set of really tiny armor?"

"Actually, that's a bottle-top spirit measure," the lady

who owned the shop said from behind the front counter. She was a nice lady, about Ginny's age, with a pleasant smile and jolly blue eyes. "You can use it to mix your drinks."

"Ah." Mike nodded and put the thing down. "Not much of a drinker, I'm afraid."

"Huh," Haley said, inspecting a case filled with sparkling jewelry. "I'd have expected the opposite from a military guy."

"Nah. Never saw much point in getting drunk and acting stupid. It gets old after a while."

Haley glanced at him over her shoulder. "Party too much with Jared in your youth?"

He smiled. "We did have our moments, like I said. But those days are long gone. He's really, really happy with your sister. Happier than I've ever seen him, actually. Settling down and marriage agree with him."

"But not you?" She straightened.

"I'm not really Prince Charming material anymore." He tugged at his sleeve in a motion to hide the scars on his arm. He didn't like to talk about them, much less point them out to people. But still, there was something about Haley that made him want to open up to her.

"Why do you say that?" she asked, turning the tables on him. "You look fine to me."

"What?" he hedged, knowing it was pointless. "Let's

forget I brought it up, okay? Or you brought it up. What-ever. I don't like to talk about the past."

"Guess we have one thing in common then."

Mike nudged her shoulder with his as he passed by her to inspect a wall of old, rusty tools. "We've got more than that in common. What about Jared and Kendra? And don't forget your crazy obsession with someone trying to sabotage the wedding."

"Don't think you're off the hook with that, buddy." She joined him in front of a nasty-looking saw, her pink lips twitching into a smile. "I've still got my doubts about you."

"Same here," he said, though he caught her eye, and they both grinned. "Okay, maybe not so much anymore. I know you love Kendra and want her to be happy."

"I do. And there haven't been any more incidents. Maybe I *was* overreacting," Haley said.

"Let's hope." Mike's face softened. "I think it's nice that you care so much about your sister. But maybe you deserve a little happiness for yourself too."

"I'm happy," she said, though the words rang a bit hollow to his ear. Her smile dimmed, and she moved around him, her body brushing the back of his and sending sweet shivers of awareness through him. She was about a foot and a half shorter than him but curvy in all the right places. Despite their height difference, she'd fit him just fine.

And where the heck did that thought come from?

Mike shook his head and scowled. He was definitely not looking to hook up with Haley Connors or anybody else this week. He was here to support Jared. End of story. No matter how cute Haley might look in her T-shirt and shorts, and no matter how nice she smelled—like lemons and lavender. And especially no matter how soft her skin felt when it brushed against his.

Nope. No affairs for him. Not now. With all his scars and all the issues that he sensed simmering below her surface, that was just asking for trouble. And Mike had experienced enough trouble already to last him a lifetime.

The bells above the front door jangled and an older guy walked in, shorter and stout, with a white beard and a weathered, craggy face. If Mike didn't know better, he'd think he was looking at the guy from the Gordon's Fish Sticks bag. The older man walked over to the counter to chat with the shop owner, and Mike caught up to Haley near a row of old bookshelves stuffed with books and knickknacks.

"So, you're all good with the wedding stuff then?" he asked, searching for some topic of conversation. Seemed whenever he was around Haley, his mind turned into a vacuous swirl of giddy emotions. Which was totally not cool and totally not like him at all. Probably because it had been too long since he'd had a girlfriend. Yep. That had to be it. That was the excuse he was going with anyway. "We can stop at the store and get the decorations you need on the way back to the inn."

"Great, thanks for reminding me." Haley graced him with a small grin, and his day suddenly brightened. "Do you like to read?"

"Sure." He shrugged. "Never miss the sports section of the Sunday paper."

"Funny. I mean actual books. You know, like Tolstoy or *Moby Dick*."

He scrunched his nose. "Does Dan Brown count?"

"Heathen." She laughed and traced her fingers down the spines of the dusty tomes. Nice fingers, he noted. Long and tapered, with pretty pink nails.

Since when did he get giddy over a girl's fingernails? Mike coughed, annoyed that his thoughts were running away with him. "What do you read, Haley? Only serious literature, I suppose."

"Nah, I actually read all kinds of things." She leaned in, her warm breath ghosting his neck. "And I'll tell you a secret. I'm a Dan Brown fan myself. Don't tell anyone."

"Your secret's safe with me." He clenched his hands at his sides to keep from pulling her closer against him.

What the heck was wrong with him? He hadn't gone this gaga over a woman since...

Well, he couldn't remember another time, to be honest. Whatever it was that Courtney and he had had together, it had never come close to a fraction of the yearning he felt whenever Haley was close by. But it was still a horrible idea. This week was about Jared and Kendra, not him getting involved with the last person he should ever consider having an affair with.

They were too wrong for each other, too different. Not to mention they lived in two different states. Long-distance relationships never worked out. Add in his job as a pharmaceutical representative in Sioux Falls that he loved and her job in Nebraska and...

"What is it you do again?" he asked.

"For work, you mean?"

"Yeah."

"Oh, well, I'm not sure I ever told you." She picked up a delicate china cup and checked the price then set it down again. "I'm a schoolteacher. Sixth and seventh grades."

"Ah."

"Ah?"

He grinned. "That explains why you're so bossy."

Her flat look was the visual equivalent of a rude gesture. "You want bossy? I'll give you bossy, mister. Get your butt out the door so we can get those decorations and get back to the inn." She pushed him toward the exit. "I want to take a nap before the rehearsal dinner tonight."

"Yes, ma'am," he said, holding the door open for her. The sunshine beat down on his back and caused the puckered skin on his scars to sting a bit even through his clothes, but he didn't mind at all as he and Haley made their way toward the store on the corner. In fact, he'd barely thought about the past or the day Jared saved his life or anything bad at all the entire time he'd been with Haley today.

CHAPTER TEN

*T*he rehearsal dinner was more than Haley could have hoped for. They held it out on the patio, the lanterns she and Mike had put back up glowing brightly. The stars twinkled above. The smell of salt air mingled with the floral scent of the freshly cut roses and honeysuckle that spilled from the vases in the middle of the tables. Fireflies flickered magically in the field beside the inn. The breeze had died down, and it was a perfectly still summer night punctuated by the sounds of crickets and the distant waves crashing on the beach below.

Haley found herself seated next to Mike at the table. Much as she hated to admit it, she'd really enjoyed their afternoon together. After the antique shop, they'd walked through the rest of the small town, then stopped at a café for a couple of delicious strawberry-banana smoothies.

He'd even helped her pick out the decorations, miniature angels for each place setting—a special touch Haley had wanted to add in memory of their parents. She'd always told Kendra they were angels now looking down at them.

She glanced up at the stars, her eyes stinging. *I did the best job I could, Mom and Dad. I hope you forgive me.*

"Something wrong?" The concern in Mike's voice made Haley's heart squeeze.

She turned to and looked at him through her primped and curled midnight-black lashes and couldn't help admiring the easy manner he had with people. Even though he apparently had no idea of the extent of his charm, he drew people in like moths to a flame with his genuine smile and kind words. And in his black polo shirt and crisp khakis, he looked even more handsome than usual.

She could see where he'd gotten his reputation as a ladies' man in his younger days. Now, though, there seemed to be a reserve about him. She supposed that probably had to do with his accident in the military and the scars that were barely visible above his collar and down his left arm from beneath the hem of his short sleeve. He seemed self-conscious of them, but Haley couldn't see why. They were more interesting than disfiguring. Her fingers itched to reach out and touch the shiny pink areas, to soothe them, to let him know that they didn't make a difference, not to her anyway.

But they weren't nearly close enough for her to do that or even ask him about what caused his scars or for him to voluntarily tell her the stories of his past. And even though she'd told him a little bit about her parents and why she wanted angels for the table, she'd been brief, not wanting to get too deep into the hurt and angst of those early times. Even with what little she'd told him, the flash of sympathy she'd seen in his eyes had set off warning bells. It wouldn't do to discuss something so personal with a stranger. When it came down to it, they'd merely shared a couple of fun hours together, that was all. Nothing more.

She gave him a wan smile. "No, everything is great."

"So, what did you do this afternoon, sis?" Kendra, seated on her other side, asked. She had a mischievous glint in her eyes as she elbowed Haley in the arm. Her sister knew exactly where Haley had been because she'd been waiting for her outside her door at the inn when she and Mike had gotten back a few hours ago. "Did you have fun?"

"It was fine. Nice." Haley dodged the question. Mike was a good guy, she'd decided. Her earlier suspicions about him were unfounded. He was probably right about the incidents being coincidence too. Nothing more had happened, so she must have been overreacting.

Perhaps there could have been something between them if they didn't live so far apart. But they did live in two different states, and there was no getting around that. She shrugged and sipped her crisp, cold white wine spritzer, looking down at the few scraps of dinner left on her plate.

Reid Callahan, the caterer for the event, clicked on a mic at the front of the room and tapped it several times to get their attention. "Thanks, everyone, for coming tonight. I hope you enjoyed the buffet." He gestured toward the row of covered silver warming dishes against the far wall filled with lobster, sirloin steak tips, baked chicken breasts, and an array of steamed veggies and mashed potatoes. The wedding party cheered. The food had been delicious. Stacy was a lucky woman to have a man who looked like a cover model and cooked like a dream.

"Great to hear, folks." Reid chuckled. "Up next, I've been asked to run a mock first dance for the bride and groom and wedding party. So, since the DJ isn't here tonight, I'll just cue up the music here on the sound system, and we'll get on with it."

He turned off the mic then walked over to the stereo

in the corner to play the sappy country song Jared and Kendra had chosen for their first dance as husband and wife. She'd heard the song so many times on the radio now, Haley could sing it in her sleep. It was pretty and sweet and catchy enough to get in one's head and stay there indefinitely.

While Jared led her sister out onto the dance floor amid a chorus of whoops and wolf whistles, Haley sat back in her seat, wine glass in hand, to watch.

"They look good together, don't they?" Mike asked, his arm brushing hers and sending a shiver of heat through her nerve endings. "They've been taking ball-room lessons."

"Yeah, I know. Kendra told me." She laughed. "Said she was glad when her toes went numb because Jared kept stepping on them. Most guys have two left feet."

"Hey, now," he said, grinning. "There you go again with those crazy assumptions."

"Are you saying you know how to dance?" Haley arched a brow.

"All right, folks," Reid said, returning to the dance floor, mic in hand. "Now let's get the best man and maid of honor out here too."

Mike stood and extended a hand to Haley. "I'm saying some things are better done than said."

Despite the warning bells in her head saying she

should let well enough alone and keep her distance from this man for the rest of the week, Haley took his hand and followed him out onto the dance floor. Jared and Kendra and everyone else in the wedding party watched them, and Haley's skin prickled under the scrutiny, while Mike seemed to take it all in stride. Wasn't like they had a choice. This was part of the rehearsal, a requirement. He did, she noticed, turn so his scarred side was facing the ocean, away from view of the others.

After leading her in a slow waltz box step, Mike pulled her closer, and darn if her knees didn't wobble slightly at the feel of his muscular chest brushing hers. And the way he held her? As if she were both delicate and precious. It was enough to make a poor girl swoon. Not that Haley was the swooning type.

His calloused hands felt warm and strong as he swayed them in a slow waltz. His blue eyes looked darker in the candlelight of the conservatory, and his minty breath, tinged with a hint of wine from dinner, ghosted the tiny hairs near her temples, making her shudder.

"Is this okay?" he asked, his deep voice laced with concern.

"Fine." She looked away fast for fear he'd see the pleasure she had in letting someone else take control for a while. It had been too long since she'd been with a man who took charge, who treated her like a lady, who made her want to curl up against him and share all her woes. Not that she'd do that with Mike. She'd just met him, for goodness' sake. The idea was crazy, insane... yet so incredibly *appealing*.

Mind whirling, she lost track of the steps and tripped over her own feet. Luckily, Mike's strong arms were there to catch her. Fresh embarrassment stormed Haley's face. "Sorry."

"No problem." His hand on her back rubbed gently. "You're really tense. Relax. It's just you and me out here. Nothing to worry about, no one to impress."

Except when she glanced around, all eyes were still on them, including Kendra's. Her sister's gaze was a bit too knowing for Haley's comfort, and she stopped abruptly, stepping out of Mike's arms. "I think I need some air."

"Sure. Want me to come with you?" he asked, ever the gentleman.

"No, no." She forced a smile. "Stay here and have a good time with your friends. I won't be long."

She could feel the weight of his stare as she made her way to the more secluded part of the patio near the conservatory. A cool breeze blew in off the ocean, and the black-velvet sky twinkled with stars. The sound of crickets chirping and the smell of honeysuckle and roses helped calm her nerves.

"Everything all right, sis?" Kendra asked from the doorway. "Mike said you weren't feeling well."

"I'm fine." She glanced back at her sister over her shoulder. "Just a little warm."

"Mike really is a great guy, you know. Loyal, kind, great with kids. If his scars worry you, I've seen them, and they aren't nearly as bad as he makes them out to be."

"What? No. I don't mind them at all." Haley turned around. The thought of Mike being embarrassed about his looks broke her heart. He was gorgeous, maybe even more so because of the damage. The scars marked him as a survivor. In fact, in her eyes, they only made him more handsome and intriguing. They spoke of pain endured and hardship overcome. Haley knew Mike must have emotional scars to go with the physical one, and she guessed that those emotional scars were not unlike her own. Not that she'd spent a lot of time thinking about that. Nope. Not at all. "It's fine. He's fine."

"Yes, he is," Kendra teased. "C'mon, sis. What is it? He's perfect for you."

Exactly. That was what worried Haley the most. Mike was almost too perfect, which meant there was another shoe to fall. Something had to go wrong. And when that other shoe did fall, her hope was not to get crushed when it came crashing down. Still, she didn't want to tell Kendra that. Not tonight. So instead, she shrugged and tried to play it off. "I'm just not looking for a relationship right now, that's all. Besides, he lives in South Dakota and I'm in Nebraska. Logistics is a problem."

"Only if you make it one. You're a teacher. Those skills are portable and in demand. Or Mike can move too if things work out. He's a pharmaceutical rep. That's something he can do pretty much anywhere." Kendra raised her wine glass in a toast. "Here's to taking chances."

Before she could finish though, a strong gust of wind blew, and the glass flew out of her sister's hand, almost as if it had been snatched away by an unseen hand, and the delicate glass smashed down on the stone patio blocks beneath their feet.

"Well, that was weird," Kendra said, staring wide-eyed at the shards around her feet.

"I'll say." Haley rushed to the conservatory door. "Stay here. I'll be back with a new glass for you and a broom to sweep that up."

Kendra nodded, and Haley went back inside and headed down the hall to the kitchen. Since the dinner was being catered, and Stacy was out on the patio with Reid, there wasn't really anyone around to ask where things were. She began searching cabinets and cupboards for wine glasses and finally found some on the very top shelf, but even standing on tiptoe, she couldn't reach them.

Frustrated, she was just about ready to go in search of a stepladder when a familiar voice said, "Need some help?"

Mike.

Senses on high alert, Haley looked back at him over her shoulder and smiled, not missing the slow once-over he gave her backside as she stretched up on her toes as high as she could go. Molten warmth spread outward from her middle to her extremities. She thought about the first day on the patio when he'd helped her with the lights. It had bugged her then. She'd felt that somehow his helping was making fun of her being height challenged. Now it didn't bug her at all. In fact, it was kind of nice.

"Here." He moved in behind her, trapping her between the counter and his warm, muscled body as he easily reached up and snagged one of the glasses. "Let me get that for you."

As his arm brushed against her side and his breath fanned her face, all Haley could think about was how close he was. Close enough for her to see his soft lips, the dark length of his thick lashes, the hint of stubble beneath the smooth surface of his chiseled jaw. Only millimeters separated them now. If she leaned in a little bit closer, she could kiss him and...

BOOM!

All the lights went out, plunging them into darkness.

"What's going on?" Haley asked, startled out of her reverie and tensing against him.

"Not sure." Mike set the glass on the counter, his frown deepening as he turned slowly to look down the dark hall behind him. "Stay here, and I'll go find out."

"BLAST IT!" Ginny was in the library working on the books and sneaking peeks out to the patio to make sure the rehearsal dinner was going well when the lights went off. Angry, she slid off her glasses and pushed away from the table. "What the heck is wrong now?"

She glanced out at the patio. It had been lit up so pretty earlier with the lanterns, but now there was nothing. Fumbling her way through the pitch black of the moonless night, she made her way toward the kitchen, pausing halfway at the sound of someone crashing into something in the direction of the dining room. The air was filled with murmured voices and the occasional laugh from one of the confused wedding party guests.

She also heard Reid's calm, confident voice and was

infinitely grateful for him to keep things on the patio under control while she checked out what was wrong. Ginny headed for the dining room, a cold chill surrounding her.

Looking around in the darkness, she whispered, "Dooley, is that you? Is this your doing?"

No answer. Was she actually starting to believe in the ghost? Was it silly to expect him to answer?

What the heck, she had nothing to lose. She tried again. "Dooley, I don't know what you want from me. I put the shakers where you wanted, and you said if I did that then you'd help me. If you're a man of your word, then you won't ruin my first event here at the inn!"

Silence.

Disappointment coursed through her. Of course, Dooley wasn't real, and even if he was, she couldn't expect him to magically turn the lights on to help her. She chided herself for being so fanciful. She had an inn to run and a business to save.

Ginny sighed and started out of the dining room, only to be halted by the sound of a deep man's voice behind her. "Very well, but it is not *I* who cut the lights. I will see what I can do for a remedy, but I think you should look at the southwest corner of the house for the true culprit."

Frozen with fright, Ginny didn't move a muscle as

another whoosh of cold air rushed around her, and suddenly every candle they'd put out in the inn for the ceremony burst into flame, casting the whole place in warm, golden light.

Delighted gasps and clapping sounded from the wedding party on the patio, along with exclamations of "Oh, how romantic!" and "So cool! How did they do that?"

Limbs shaking and breath rapid, Ginny grabbed a flashlight from one of the drawers in the dining room and headed straight for the location Dooley had given her. At the southwest corner of the building, her heart dropped to her toes.

The electrical box was open and the wires cut.

She'd been starting to think all the little things that had gone wrong were just coincidence, but now she knew for sure.

Someone did not want this wedding to happen.

CHAPTER ELEVEN

*W*hile she waited in the dark kitchen alone, Haley had some time to think. She'd been a fool to let her guard down and assume that the other incidents had been just flukes. This power outage could not be coincidence. The night was clear, and other than the odd gust of wind that had taken Kendra's wine glass, there was no reason for power to go out. Nope, now she was certain someone was trying to put a damper on the wedding.

And given that Mike had been with her when the power went out, there was only one inevitable conclusion. He couldn't have been the one trying to sabotage the wedding. Unless he had an accomplice, which seemed unlikely.

As she stood there contemplating who else it might

be, a glow passed by the window behind the sink—a flashlight. The saboteur? On instinct, Haley followed. Mike had told her to stay put, but she didn't care. Besides, Mike would want her to find out who was trying to mess up his best friend's wedding, right?

Silently, she slipped out the side door and tiptoed in the direction the light had traveled moments earlier. Down the side of the house and around the corner and—

She nearly ran right over someone. A startled squeak stopped Haley in her tracks, her heart pounding loud enough to be heard across the Atlantic. The beam from a flashlight swung up to her face, blinding her.

"Oh, my gosh. You scared me half to death," Ginny said, pointing the light back at the side of the house. "What are you doing out here?"

"I saw your light through the kitchen window and came to investigate." Haley blinked her eyes several times to get rid of the spots dancing before them then squinted. On the side of the inn was a rat's nest of wires coming from the telephone pole and going into a conduit. One of the wires, though, was hanging out of the conduit, the other end dangling from the pole. "Did that wire snap?"

"Looks that way," Ginny said, taking Haley's arm and pulling her back as one of the cables sparked and jumped. "We're going to have to block off this area until the power company can get out here to repair them. I just can't understand how this could happen."

"Hey, what's going on out here?" Mike jogged up behind Haley. "Anything I can help with?"

"Not unless you're Central Maine Power." Ginny shook her head and pointed at the dangling wires. "The wiring is old. Maybe I should have had it rewired before now."

"That's weird." Mike scowled, his face lit by the faint glow of candlelight from the nearby window. "There's not much wind tonight. Seems odd for the wires to come down on their own. Can I see your flashlight?"

Ginny handed it over, and Haley followed Mike over to the telephone pole. A few more sparks zapped on the dangling wire, and Mike put out his hand to keep Haley safe. Her heart swelled annoyingly at his thoughtfulness.

"Ginny, you might want to call the power company now. They should have a twenty-four-hour hotline for emergencies. Not sure if they can reattach the lines tonight, but they should at least be able to cut the main power source at the transformer so no one gets electrocuted."

"Good thinking." Ginny headed toward the side door. "Be right back."

Mike scrubbed his hand over his face as he aimed the

beam at the wire. "This wire didn't just come down on its own."

"No?" Haley moved in beside him, doing her best to ignore the thump of her heart at his nearness. They were here to solve a mystery, not cuddle. "How do you know?"

Mike shook his head. "How could it? Wires just don't snap no matter how old they are, and when they do, they don't snap in a clean cut like this one."

"Someone cut it? But how could they do that? Wouldn't they get electrocuted?"

"Not if they used insulated wire cutters." Mike swept the flashlight over the ground as if looking for the offending tool.

Haley stared up at the box then back at the dangling wire. "Wow. Guess this takes our sabotage theory to a whole new level, huh?"

"Seems so." Mike straightened alongside Haley. "Who in the wedding party would have insulated wire cutters, though?"

"Good question."

"And who wasn't around when the power went out?"

"Another good question. But we were in the kitchen. I have no idea if someone snuck away from the party."

Ginny returned, and Haley forced a smile she didn't quite feel. If whoever wanted this wedding called off had resorted to cutting electrical wires, things were definitely getting more serious.

"Did you get a hold of the power company?" Haley asked.

"Yes," Ginny said. "They're sending a truck now to see what they can do tonight."

"That's good." Mike gestured for Ginny to come closer. "I want to show you this before the workmen remove it. There's a clean cut on this wire. Meaning it didn't come down by itself. Someone helped it along." He straightened, wincing slightly. Haley felt the insane urge to rush to his side and comfort him but refrained. "Listen, Haley and I have both been doing some investigation around here over the past few days. We think someone might be trying to sabotage Jared and Kendra's wedding."

"What? Oh my!" Ginny placed her hand on her chest. "I hope you don't think my employees or I had anything to do with this."

"No, no." Mike gave her a reassuring smile, patting her on the shoulder. "We think it's probably someone within the wedding party."

"Oh. Well, I wouldn't be so sure." Ginny stared down at the branch. "Truthfully, I've had my share of strange things happening around here well before you and your party got here. This could have nothing to do with the wedding at all. It could be about me."

"You?" Haley slid an arm around the older woman, giving her an incredulous look. "No. Who would possibly want to put you out of business? This inn is lovely and you're a sweetheart. I can't imagine anyone wanting to harm you or this place."

Haley glanced at Mike. She had been thinking it was someone in the wedding party, namely him. But what if it wasn't one of them? Though she couldn't imagine any of the nice people involved with the inn doing this. Then again, most of them had not been out on the patio during the dinner because Reid had been catering it, so none of the staff from the inn were needed.

"Well, either way, I'm not going to let them ruin my best friend's wedding," Mike said, moving in on Ginny's other side. "We're going to find out who's responsible and put a stop to it, once and for all."

"Thank you both for the solidarity." Ginny smiled. "Now, I best get inside and make an announcement to the rest of the guests about what's going on."

"Okay, but let's not let on that we think someone is behind it. I wouldn't want Kendra or Jared to get nervous, thinking someone was maliciously trying to ruin things for them," Haley said.

"Yeah, and we don't want to tip our hand. It's better

if the person thinks no one is watching. That will make it easier to catch them," Mike said.

"Okay, sure, that sounds like it would be best all around. I'll just tell them a gust of wind snapped the old wire." Ginny turned and headed back to the inn.

Mike and Haley stayed outside, dappled candlelight seeping through the windows to shadow the area.

"So," Haley said, feeling suddenly shy. "Guess we're on the same side now."

"Guess so." Mike winked at her then took her hand, lacing their fingers together. "And since we're a team, there's no getting past us anymore."

AN HOUR LATER, the power company had a cherry-picker truck on-site to fix the lines while all the inn's guests gathered in the backyard around a huge bonfire. Mike sat near the back of the group with Haley, her bare leg occasionally brushing against his and drawing his attention back to how soft she was. She hadn't stared at his scars either, not once this entire week. And during the time they'd spent together, she hadn't seemed to care about them at all. It was almost enough to give a guy hope someone might still want him despite his issues.

Someone like Haley. She was funny and smart and beautiful.

Not only that, but she had a sensitive side even though she tried to hide it. He'd seen it when they'd picked out the angel decorations. She'd acted like her parents' death was something she'd come to terms with, but he'd sensed that it still cut her deeply. You just didn't "come to terms" with trauma like that. Mike should know. He understood why she didn't want to talk about it. Same reason he never wanted to talk about how he got his scars or how it had affected his life and his relationships afterward. But he got a feeling that if there was ever anyone who would understand how he felt, it would be Haley.

She was everything he'd ever wanted and nothing he deserved.

Add in the fact he knew for certain she wasn't involved in sabotaging the wedding and she seemed damned near perfect to him. Maybe once they got the wedding sorted, he'd consider asking her out.

Haley shivered beside him, and Mike glanced over at her, concerned. "You cold?"

"Nah, I'm fine," she said, though her arms were crossed. "Looks like everyone's making the best of the outage."

"Yep." He leaned back on his elbows atop the

blanket they'd spread on the grass. People were drinking warm beer and singing campfire songs and generally having a good time. It was kind of nice, not a cell phone in sight. Haley shivered again, and he gave her a pointed look. "You should move closer to the fire."

"What about you?" she asked, frowning.

"I'm fine back here." This was about as close as he wanted to get to the flames. Too many bad memories. Flashbacks to that awful day when Jared had had to pull him from that destroyed village and save his life. He'd nearly burned to death that day. Mike never wanted to go through anything like that again. He swallowed hard and looked away. Maybe someday he would tell her all about it, but not today. "Interesting about what Ginny said, huh?"

"You mean about someone being after her instead of the wedding?" She shrugged then leaned back on her elbows too, mimicking his pose, her legs crossed in front of her. "Yeah, but I just can't understand why anyone would go after her. She's such a sweet lady. My gut tells me this is still about the wedding, not Ginny."

"Your gut tells you that, eh?" He gave her some side eye and grinned, then laid back to stare up into the starry sky. "Well, I never thought I'd say this, Haley Connors, but I agree with you."

She flopped down on the blanket beside him and

giggled. "Wait! Let me savor this moment for a second. Mike Sanderson agrees with me. Wonders never cease."

He laughed, full and strong, like he hadn't in so long and feared he never would again. "I do. I agree with you. Achievement unlocked."

"Indeed." Haley smiled, and the simmering tension inside Mike unfurled a tad.

"Indeed," he said, feeling lighter and fuller and warmer than he had in years.

CHAPTER TWELVE

*D*espite the events of the previous night, Haley woke up more optimistic than she'd been in a long time. One more day until the wedding, and the bachelorette party was that night at a local pub called the Salty Dog. Hopefully with Mike's help she'd be able to ward off any more occurrences. Even if they didn't catch the person, they only had to make it through one and a half days.

Once she'd showered and dressed, she headed downstairs to start her busy day. Kendra might be using the inn's wedding planner for the major pieces of the ceremony and reception, but there were still a ton of smaller details that were up to Haley to oversee. Not to mention the fact that she'd have to keep her eyes open. Whoever was messing with things was certainly going to great lengths. The earlier mishaps had been just minor things. But now whoever it was seemed to be getting serious. Escalating.

As she reached the entrance to the kitchen, Haley saw Maisie at the back door. The local bakery was delivering her sister's wedding cake. After signing off on the paperwork, she carefully inspected the four-tiered, pastel pink and white confection to make sure it matched what Kendra wanted—alternating layers of pink and white frosting with the pink layers festooned with tiny iridescent pearls of frosting in a fleur-de-lis pattern and the white layers draped by thin strips of white silk chiffon garland interspersed with real red roses. The top of the whole thing was crowned with pink and white and red roses and edible pearls.

Satisfied, Haley left the cake in the capable hands of Maisie and headed outside to call the photographer. The man was a local, and Haley wanted to make an appointment so they could find some areas on the property where he could get scenic shots of the wedding party.

Haley was especially excited about this part because Kendra had been flustered about wedding pictures. She seemed to have no sense of what a good backdrop would be, and Haley wanted to pick out a few killer spots as a special surprise.

By the time she'd made her appointment for later

that day with the photographer and tended to a dozen other details, it was nearly noon, and the rest of the wedding party had already made plans and split up for the day—some going to the beach to relax, some playing croquet or volleyball in the backyard. Neither activity seemed particularly interesting to Haley, so she decided to check out the extensive gardens in the back of the inn. This was another spot the photographer had mentioned maybe taking some shots, so she could scope out the locations. Plus, it would give her a chance to mull over who might be trying to ruin Kendra's wedding.

On her way out the back, she decided to stop in the kitchen for a bottled water and found her sister and Rachel standing in front of the cake.

"Wow!" Rachel stared wide-eyed at the cake. "That's so pretty I almost hate to eat it."

"I know, right?" Kendra laughed. "They did an amazing job."

Thankfully the power was back on, and Maisie and Ginny were busy making room for the cake in the inn's walk-in refrigerator. As Haley reached past them to grab a water, Mike walked in and said a brief hello to Kendra and Rachel before heading over to Haley.

"Hey." He leaned a hip against the edge of the counter, his warm smile making her stomach do an odd little flip. "I was hoping I'd find you this morning."

"Yeah?" She watched him over the rim of her bottle as she sipped her water. "Why? What's going on?"

"Nothing." He tilted his head slightly, looking far too adorable for his own good. "I thought maybe if you weren't busy, we could talk about last night and come up with a plan for tomorrow."

"Oh." She tucked a curl that had escaped her ponytail behind her ear. "Sure, that sounds fine. I just finished up most of the stuff I had to get done today, and I have to meet the photographer, but that's later on. I was going to take a walk in the gardens out back. Want to join me?"

"Absolutely." He straightened and grinned. She glanced up at him then over at her sister and Rachel—who were watching the scene unfold with growing interest—before following him out of the kitchen. Her pulse kicked up a notch, pounding louder in her ears as Mike held the French doors in the conservatory open for her and they walked outside onto the empty patio. "Such a glorious day."

"Yeah." Haley slipped her sunglasses into place, grateful for the small barrier between her and Mike's too-perceptive gaze. She'd always been told all her emotions were easily read in her eyes, so the sunglasses were a small protection against him seeing too much.

"Did you think any more about who might have cut

that wire?" she asked once they were out of earshot of the inn.

"Yeah." He walked down the stone steps to the flat, grassy gardens below. "I talked to the guys, but no one remembers anyone leaving the party before the lights went out. Then again, no one was really paying attention, and after the lights went out, no one was able to see. What about you?"

"I've been too busy this morning to talk to anybody about it really."

"Right." Mike walked alongside her through the lush green foliage. They headed slowly down a row of rose-bushes, nothing but the distant roar of waves and the soft summer breeze surrounding them. "I've been thinking a lot about last night, actually."

"And?"

"And I'm starting to give a bit more credence to what Ginny said. Maybe it is someone after her and not a member of the wedding party. I mean, who among us would want to ruin Kendra and Jared's big day? Besides, I still can't imagine who would've brought insulated wire cutters. The other guys work at the hospital with Jared. They're doctors and paper pushers. Hardly Bob Villa types. And I can't imagine one of the bridesmaids having a pair of those. They all seem so ladylike."

"Sexist much?" Haley snorted. "You don't think a girl

could cut a wire?"

"No. I think women can do anything men can do, if they want to. But I just don't see any of the bridesmaids *knowing* how to cut a wire?"

Haley shrugged. "It's as easy as googling, right? And anyone could go into town and buy wire cutters, or if they were planning it before we came, they could have brought them. Things have been happening since the day we got here, so whoever it is most likely was planning it before we came."

"You could be right. I've googled all kinds of things like how to fix things on my car or how to rewire a lamp. There's probably a video on how to cut house wires on YouTube. And they might even have the tools here in that old shed. But if it's not someone in our group, it could be someone that knows how to cut wires. We don't know a thing about any of the people associated with the inn."

Mike's mention of the old shed brought the strange gardener to mind. "Yeah, like that gardener. I saw her watching us down on the beach when we had the bee incident."

"I think Ginny said she was new. Maybe this really is about the inn. That would be a huge relief, because I hate to think that it's any of our friends."

Haley replayed the bee incident in her head. Sure,

the gardener looking down had been weird, but something else had been weird too: the look between Rachel and Mike when she handed him the peanut-butter-and-honey sandwich. "Yeah, but things have been happening *to* Kendra. Or at least it seems that way. And that bee incident... well, how did you end up with a peanut-butter-and-honey sandwich? I saw Rachel pass it to you and got kind of a vibe."

Mike frowned. "Vibe? Simone and Rachel made sandwiches that day. Simone asked me if I wanted a peanut butter, honey, and banana sandwich—everyone knows they're my favorite. Rachel likes them too, so I guess maybe that's the vibe you thought you saw. People tease us about them."

"Hmmm, maybe I imagined it." But she hadn't imagined the vibe, and come to think of it, Rachel was flirty and had been around when all the strange things happened. Had she been on the patio just before the power was cut? "You'd think Rachel would have known not to bring honey around Kendra. She's her best friend. Surely she would know about her bee allergy."

Mike made a face. "Are you saying that you think Rachel is the culprit? Nah, she's too ditzy. Probably forgot about the allergy."

Mike slowed to a stop and turned to face her. They were in a dense, secluded part of the garden, and Haley felt the air around them change. He took her hand, and her pulse jumped.

"The real reason I wanted to come out here with you was to tell you I had a real nice time last night. Sitting on the lawn, talking and laughing."

She should've pulled her hand back, but instead Haley let him continue to hold it, his thumb rubbing lazy circles on her palm as she got lost in the bright-blue depths of his eyes. Her question emerged softer and more breathy than she wanted. "You did?"

He tugged her closer, until she stood between his spread legs, his broad chest brushing against her through the turquoise fabric of his polo shirt. "I did."

Time seemed to slow as he slid his arm around her waist to lock her in place and his head lowered toward hers. This close, she heard the slight catch in his breath as his lips hovered just out of reach then a slight brush of his mouth over hers—once, twice—before he captured her lips with his.

Breath held, Haley stood on tiptoe and remained perfectly still, afraid that if she moved at all, this moment would end, and she very, very much wanted it to continue. Mike leaned back slightly and gazed down at her through half-lidded eyes, his warm, minty breath ghosting over her face as the sun shone down from the blue sky above.

"Is this okay?" he asked, his tone low and rough.

Not trusting her voice to answer, Haley slid her hands around his neck and into the soft hair at the nape of his neck, her slow smile growing by the second. This was more than okay. This was nothing she thought she wanted and everything she needed. Nails scraping against his scalp, she pulled his head back down to hers, enjoying his slight shudder against her.

"It's fine," she whispered over his lips.

FROM THE SECOND HIS lips were on hers, all thoughts of his scars and his past and his concerns about the wedding flew from Mike's mind. It had been too long since he'd been with someone who made him feel this way, and Haley affected him like no other woman before.

His blood raced along with his heart as she gasped, and he took advantage, sliding his tongue against hers and tasting her for the first time—mint and sweetness and a hint of spice. Oh, yeah. Their chemistry was off the charts, and after last night's conversation on that blanket, they seemed compatible in a lot of other areas too. Maybe it wasn't so ridiculous to think they could make a go of it. Yes, she lived in Nebraska and he lived in South Dakota, but he traveled all the time for his job, so it wouldn't be that big a deal to work out his schedule to see her every other weekend, or more often, if it suited.

She moaned low in her throat and pressed tighter against him, and he clutched the back of her shirt like a drowning man grasping a life preserver. At this moment, she was the most real thing in the world to him, and he never wanted to let go.

Hell, he swore he even heard bells, at least until Haley finally pulled away and Mike realized it was the grandfather clock in the conservatory chiming.

As quickly as the kiss had started, it ended. Haley's chest was heaving and her lips were swollen and pink. Her eyes looked wild, and her cheeks were flushed. She stumbled back another step and said, "I'm sorry. I have to go."

Then, just like that, she was gone, leaving him alone in the gardens.

Stunned, Mike walked over to a nearby stone bench and plopped down, running a shaky hand through his hair as all his old insecurities flooded back. He'd thought he'd gotten all the right signals from Haley, but maybe she'd not wanted to kiss him. After all, being on his own for so long had left him a bit rusty in the romance department. Or maybe he'd been wrong about her not caring about his scars? Could she be freaked out by them, just like every other woman he'd met since his discharge?

And that connection he'd *thought* he'd felt between them. Had it been all in his imagination?

Mike sighed and stared up at the clear blue sky. He'd been an idiot to even dare to hope. He was about to head back into the inn when Jared's voice shouted to him through the bushes.

"Hey, Mike, man? You in there?"

Pushing to his feet, Mike wandered back out of the gardens and over to the patio where Jared stood. "What's going on?"

"We need another person for the volleyball team. You in?"

"Uh, sure. I guess." He followed Jared around the side of the house only to spot Haley, looking far too cozy with some random guy he'd not seen before. They were chatting and laughing, and Mike's gut tightened when Haley laid her hand on the guy's arm all friendly and nice. Who was the guy? Then he remembered, the guests for the wedding were starting to come to town. He was probably a guest. Maybe even a boyfriend.

Upset with himself for believing a woman like her would actually be interested in a guy like him, Mike lowered his head and followed Jared over to the edge of the yard where the volleyball net was set up.

Whatever he'd imagined between him and Haley, he should have known it was too good to be true.

CHAPTER THIRTEEN

"**C**an I get you a fresh appletini?" the bartender at the Salty Dog asked.

"Oh, no thank you." Haley nursed the same drink she'd had since arriving at the pub an hour prior. The last thing she wanted to do was drink too much at her sister's bachelorette party and make a fool out of herself. How cliché would that be?

She watched the bartender walk away then swiveled on her stool to gaze out over the rest of the bar. Kendra and the majority of her bridesmaids were out on the makeshift dance floor that had been set up in one corner of the place. The DJ was pumping out all the latest pop tunes, and the infectious rhythms even had Haley tapping her toe to the beat despite her vow to stay vigilant—in case whoever was trying to sabotage the wedding tried to do something to ruin this party.

Rowdy whoops and hollers rang out from her sister and the rest of the group of gals. She was glad they were having fun. Now, if she could just get tipsy Rachel, who was slumped on the stool beside Haley's, out on the dance floor to work off some of the alcohol, things would be marvelous.

Instead, however, Rachel seemed more than content to blabber Haley's ear off, even though she wasn't paying much attention. Nope. In fact, her mind was still squarely focused on that kiss she'd shared with Mike in the gardens earlier. *Yowza.* The man knew what he was doing in that department. In fact, her lips still tingled whenever she thought of the way his warm, soft lips had felt against hers, the way he'd tasted of mint. The way his arms had surrounded her, making her feel both protected and desired at the same time.

Haley sighed and sipped her neon-green drink. She'd gone back to find him after she'd finished up with the photographer to try and explain why she'd run away so quickly, but he'd been gone, and things had been so busy that she hadn't had a chance to seek him out.

She hoped he didn't think she had been too rude. Truth was she'd forgotten all about her appointment with the photographer until the clock chimed, then she'd panicked that she would be late. Kendra's wedding pictures were important, and she'd been able to approve of several gorgeous photo locations suggested by the photographer. Honestly, though, the photographer could've asked her if she approved of the moon being made of cream cheese at that point and she would've said yes. She'd still been that flustered from the kiss with Mike.

Mike had been playing a game in the yard with the other guys when she'd come downstairs to leave for the bachelorette party. She'd said goodbye to Mike, but he'd acted distant and cold. It was all so weird. Did Mike regret their kiss in the garden? Was that why he'd acted so standoffish? Or did he just not want to let on that something had happened in front of the other guys?

"They both dated a lot of women, you know?" Rachel slurred from beside Haley as she swayed on her stool. It was a wonder the girl was still upright, let alone managed to stay seated.

"I'm sorry?" Haley blinked patiently, wondering if Rachel would even remember any of this in the morning.

"Mike and Jared," Rachel said. "They both dated a lot of women." She leaned in closer, her booze-laced breath making Haley's nose wrinkle. "And I'm not so sure they're over that phase—or the women—if you know what I mean."

Haley's heart sank a bit. She'd thought she'd gotten past the nagging doubt that Mike was a player, but apparently she hadn't—if the tightness in her chest was any indication. "Why? What have you heard?"

"Hey, no need to go on about that now, is there?" Simone had appeared on the other side of Haley and must have overheard Rachel.

Rachel glanced up at the other girl and frowned. "Just saying it like it is," she slurred.

"Wait, do you guys know something about Jared and Mike that I should know?" Haley asked.

"No," Simone said.

"No sirree." Rachel shook her head then gripped the edge of the bar tight and squeezed her eyes shut as if the whole room was spinning. After a moment, she grinned and waved down the bartender. "Another one of these, please."

The bartender glanced at Haley and Simone, who both shook their heads.

"One more hurricane, coming up." The bartender winked and then filled a glass with water and a splash of cranberry.

Waiting until after Rachel's faux refill had arrived, Haley asked again. "What is it that you were going to say, Rachel?"

"Just that Mike and Jared like to party a lot. We've

partied with them many times. Right, Simone?" Rachel gave Simone an exaggerated wink.

"We were younger then," Simone said. "Kind of old for that lifestyle now."

Rachel shrugged and slurped her drink. "Some men never get over that lifestyle, you know? They just keep on with their player ways forever. They just want another notch in their belt. And who wants to be another notch? " Rachel looked pointedly at Simone before downing the rest of her drink.

What was that look for? Did Simone have something going on with Mike or Jared? What was Rachel trying to say?

Simone took Rachel by the arm. "Okay, kid, time to work the alcohol off." She rolled her eyes at Haley as she tugged Rachel off the stool.

Rachel stood on wobbly legs and headed for the dance floor. "Hey, we should all go down to the beach again in the morning. Sleep some of this off before the ceremony in the afternoon."

A cheer went up from the rest of the girls as Rachel stumbled toward them with Simone at her side, ready to keep her from falling. Soon, a raucous cheer of "beach, beach, beach" rose up from the wedding party. Guess that was decided then. What wasn't decided, however, was how Haley felt about being just another conquest for Mike.

Because it sounded exactly like that was what Rachel had been implying? Had she been another notch in Mike's belt?

She glanced down the bar and spotted Stacy and her fiancé Reid. They made such a nice couple, her with her honey-blond hair and his dark-brown coppery locks. They were talking and laughing and snuggling and obviously so in love that it made Haley's chest ache.

After that kiss in the garden, she'd entertained the possibility that maybe happiness like that might be possible for her and Mike too. But now, after his cold-shoulder treatment back at the house and what Rachel had just said, Haley had serious doubts. Maybe she'd been right all along and love just wasn't in the cards for her.

Haley was so absorbed in her thoughts that she didn't notice Reid heading back into the kitchens and Stacy heading over to talk to her.

"Anyone sitting here?" Stacy asked, pointing to the stool Rachel had recently vacated.

"No." Haley forced a weak smile as the bartender cleared away the empty glasses.

"That power outage was freaky at the inn, huh?" Stacy said as the bartender brought her a glass of white wine. "I can honestly say that's never happened before, at least not since I've been there. And I can't believe

Ginny said someone deliberately cut the line too. Who would do that?"

A bit shocked that Ginny shared that information, Haley shrugged. "Not sure."

Stacy leaned in closer, her voice low. "I know not to mention it to anyone else. But Ginny told me you and Mike were there and that Mike's the one who discovered the line had been cut deliberately."

"Yep." A new song started on the speaker system. This one had a thumping beat even louder than the others. There was no way anyone would be able to over-hear their conversation, so Haley felt a bit more relaxed about opening up and discussing what they'd learned so far. "Yeah, Mike and I have sort of teamed up to find the culprit. There's been other things happening that are suspicious too." She shared the fallen lanterns and the bee at the beach. "Thankfully, my sister didn't have to use her EpiPen that day. Those things are crazy expensive."

"No doubt." Stacy sipped her wine, her expression thoughtful. "I still can't imagine who would want to ruin things for your sister or for Ginny though. They're both so nice and sweet."

"Me neither. That's the problem. With the wedding tomorrow, I really need to get to the bottom of who's doing these things. I won't have my sister's wedding ruined."

"No, I totally get that." Stacy ran a finger around the rim of her wine glass, frowning. "You know, there's one person who'd have access to tools like that and who no one would think twice about seeing them lurk around the side of the house and whose absence on the patio that night wouldn't have been noticed."

"Who?"

"The new gardener Ginny hired. Her name's Emery Santos."

"Yes, the dark-haired girl." Was Mike right and whoever was behind this was not with the wedding? Haley hoped so. She hated to think of how disappointed Kendra would be to discover one of her friends was trying to ruin things for her.

"Yep." Stacy sighed. "I like her, I really do, but she's very quiet and keeps to herself a lot. I'm not accusing her of anything, but there sure seem to be a lot of pieces that fit the puzzle there, huh?"

"Yeah." Haley scowled, remembering that day at the beach. Maybe this Emery person did have something to do with all the mishaps around the inn. But why? And did it have anything to do with the wedding? What if this Emery person was one of the notches on Jared's belt that Rachel had been talking about? But surely someone would have recognized her. Then again, come to think of it, she kept to herself. Haley had only glimpsed her a few times. Maybe no one else had seen her.

It sounded like she might be a little weird, too. Weird enough to follow them out here and pose as a gardener to ruin the wedding? That seemed a little far-fetched. She decided to press a bit farther to see what she could find out from Stacy. "When did Emery start?"

Stacy pressed her lips together. "About two weeks ago."

Two weeks? They'd been planning the wedding for months, and the location was no secret. If someone were devious enough, they could have come out and gotten a job... But someone would have to be a real sicko to go to all that trouble. Goosebumps chased up Haley's arm. There was no telling what lengths a person who was that determined to ruin a wedding would go to.

"I'm sure Ginny screens all of her employees thoroughly before hiring them, right?" Haley said.

"She does." Stacy smiled. "But she also seems to have a soft spot for people with problems. Just look at me."

"You?" Haley chuckled. "Your life looks pretty perfect to me."

"It wasn't always. Before I came back home to Boulder Point, I was a real workaholic. Fast-paced job, fast-paced life. Then I came here for my dad's funeral and reconnected with my past and with Reid." Her pretty face lit up at the mention of her husband-to-be. "And the rest is history."

"Wow. That sounds like the hand of fate."

"It does. Ginny definitely played a hand in all that too. She took me under her wing, which is what she's doing for Emery now. She's even letting her live at the inn for free until she gets back on her feet again." Stacy's lips tightened into a thin line. "But I'm not sure Ginny looked into her references too deeply."

"Then why would she want to make trouble for Ginny?" Haley asked, confused.

"Your guess is as good as mine," Stacy said, sliding off her stool. "I need to get back home. See you later."

CHAPTER FOURTEEN

*I*t was after midnight by the time Haley and the other gals got back to the inn. From the raucous laughter and taunts issuing from the library, the guys' poker game was still in full swing.

"I'm gonna go in and say goodnight to Jared," Kendra said, still tipsy from the bar. "You guys coming?"

"Shhhure!" Rachel tripped and would have fallen if not for Haley catching her.

"I think someone needs to go to their room." Simone grabbed Rachel's arm and tugged her toward the stairs.

"You need help?" Georgia asked as Rachel sagged against Simone.

"Nah, I can carry her if I have to. One good thing about nursing, you get strong lifting patients."

"Yeah." Rachel perked up, hanging on to the banister

as Simone helped her up the steps. "Remember how we lifted that really really really really fat guy onto the gurney ourselves that time?"

"Yep. Watch it here on the landing."

"They'll be okay," Kendra said, glancing up at the top of the stairs, where Simone was now practically carrying Rachel. "Let's go see how the poker game is going."

The others turned toward the library, but Haley hung back. Considering the chilly reception she'd gotten from Mike earlier, she didn't think a repeat was such a good idea. She headed toward the stairs instead. "Nah, you girls go ahead. I'm going to turn in. Big day tomorrow."

When Haley got to the top of the steps, she saw Simone holding Rachel up in front of the door to her room at the end of the hall. She turned and waved, then backed into the room with Rachel in tow.

Haley opened her own door. Rachel sure was going to have a hangover tomorrow, but hopefully she'd recover in time for the wedding. Haley brushed her teeth and laid out her pink cotton pajamas then decided she was too ramped up for sleeping. Chamomile tea might do the trick.

Not wanting to deal with the crowd that still sounded boisterous in the library, she quietly walked down the front stairs and navigated the hall to the kitchen. She turned on one low light over the stove to heat her kettle of water, then went in search of teabags and milk. She'd seen some at breakfast this morning, so they had to be around here somewhere. In the dim light, it was hard to tell the difference between the tall cabinets and the door to the walk-in fridge.

Once the door to the cooler was open, however, it wasn't hard to see at all with the bright light that came on automatically. She squinted and blinked several times to clear her vision, then she stopped short, her heart jerking in her chest.

Kendra's gorgeous wedding cake lay in pieces all over the shelf where it sat, carved apart in big, jagged, unrepairable chunks.

Haley clutched the doorframe of the fridge, her knees unsteady—this time from alarm, not booze. She didn't remember making a noise, but suddenly Ginny was at her side.

"What's going on, dear?" She peeked past Haley into the walk-in fridge then gasped. "Oh, no! Who would do such a thing?"

Closing the door quickly on the confectionary carnage, Haley leaned back against the fridge and held her stomach. "The same person who cut the wire, the same person who wants to stop this wedding."

"I swear that cake was fine an hour ago, Haley."

Ginny slumped down into one of the kitchen chairs. "I came in here to fix myself some coffee before I went into the study next door to work. I didn't hear anyone enter or leave until you girls came back." She exhaled, her shoulders dropping.

"Well, it couldn't have been any of the bridesmaids," Haley said. "We just got here, and everyone is either in the library with the guys or upstairs."

Haley's mind replayed the conversation with Stacy. She'd said the gardener, Emery, lived on-site at the inn, free of charge. If she kept to herself as much as Stacy seemed to think she did, then chances were Emery would've been here. Could she have snuck down to the kitchen and destroyed the cake when no one was looking?

She still couldn't understand why Emery would do such a thing though. What possible motive could she have?

None of it made sense. Worse, those ragged stab marks on the beautiful cake looked violent and brutal, signifying someone with a lot more problems than just wanting to halt a wedding. Another round of boisterous laughter erupted from the library, and Haley squeezed her eyes shut. Could it be one of the groomsmen? They had been here the whole time.

"Please don't tell anyone what's happened," Haley

said to Ginny. The last thing she wanted was for Kendra to see her gorgeous cake ruined like that. "I'll go to the bakery first thing in the morning and see if there's any way they can redo it in time for the reception."

"I'll do you one better." Ginny stood, her expression determined. "Let me handle the bakery. The owner's a friend of mine. I'll call first thing and get you all fixed up with something as close to the original as possible. Okay?"

For the first time since opening the fridge accidentally, Haley felt a bit of the weight on her shoulders lifting. "More than okay. Thank you."

CHAPTER FIFTEEN

*G*iven what she'd seen in the fridge the night before, Haley didn't sleep well. On top of it all was the added pressure of the impending wedding ceremony and reception that evening and the fact that her sister and Jared were leaving early the next morning for their honeymoon. All of it left her in a tangled mess of stress. At least once it was all over, she wouldn't have to worry anymore. But until her sister and Jared were legally wed and safely on their way to Barbados, she needed to be extra cautious.

Once she'd showered and dressed, Haley went downstairs and found Ginny in the kitchen along with Maisie and Mike. The sight of him made her stomach flip. He hadn't made any attempt to talk to her since the kiss. In fact, it seemed like he was avoiding her. Probably didn't want her to get too attached so he could go on his way, putting more notches on his belt. Obviously whatever connection she'd thought they'd made had been in her imagination.

"Good morning," Ginny said as Haley walked in. "Sit down and let me fix you a plate for breakfast. What would you like? Maisie made some incredible French toast with fresh whipped cream and strawberries."

"Sounds perfect." Haley took the chair opposite Mike and did her best to avoid his gaze. "Were you able to contact your friend at the bakery this morning?"

"I was," Ginny said as she dished up food onto a plate. "It's not a problem at all. We caught them during a downtime. The new cake will be delivered for the reception."

"New cake?" Mike asked, frowning. "What happened to the old one?"

After glancing around to make sure no one else was lurking about, Haley quietly told him what she'd found in the walk-in fridge the previous evening. She was going to leave it at that. They weren't partners in this anymore, but she found herself blurting out her suspicions. "I hate to say it, but my suspicions are leaning toward the gardener, Emery. Stacy told me last night she's very quiet and keeps to herself, but she has a toolshed full of tools and might know how to cut electrical wires. Plus, I saw her near the beach that day when the bee incident occurred. I was wondering if maybe she knows Jared or Kendra from before somehow."

Mike made a face as if he thought she was being ridiculous. It did sound kind of ridiculous that the gardener would coincidentally have a grudge against Kendra or Jared. But his face only solidified her feelings that anything between her and Mike was purely fiction. If Mike really did care about her, he would at least consider her suspicions.

"Here you are." Ginny set Haley's plate down on the table. "What are you two whispering about?"

Heat prickled Haley's cheeks. She wasn't a person who enjoyed gossiping about others, and Stacy had said how fond Ginny was of Emery, but they had to find out if the gardener was capable of sabotaging her sister's wedding. "I was just asking Mike if he'd met your new gardener, Emery."

"Oh, my. Well, Emery's a quiet little thing. Very polite though, and smart. Has a master's degree in horticulture too. She's done a beautiful job with my landscaping, and I feel lucky to have found her. Why?"

Throat constricted, Haley forced herself to swallow a bite of French toast. "She'd have access to tools, right?"

"I suppose so." Ginny frowned. "There's a whole shed full of tools out back."

Mike crossed his arms, his expression disgusted. "What Haley's trying to imply is that maybe this Emery person is responsible for cutting the wire the other night."

Haley glared at him across the table. So much for tact.

"Emery?" Ginny scoffed. "No. She'd never do anything like that. I'd vouch for her myself. Why, she even lives here, under my roof. She takes great care of the gardens, the birdbaths, and she's even reviving the old beehives out back. She's a good girl."

"See?" Mike shook his head, giving Haley a flat stare. "Just another dead end. And it could've been anyone who ruined that cake too. What possible motive could the gardener have for doing it?"

Annoyed by him pointing out the obvious, Haley did the same to him. "It couldn't have been just anyone. You said it yourself. It had to be someone with the ability to plan and slip away from the party unnoticed to cut the wires *or* be someone who wasn't at the party in the first place. Given the time frame when the cake was attacked, it would've been close to impossible for someone to drive out here, butcher the cake, then leave again with no one seeing or hearing anything. Which means it was most likely someone already here at the inn. That leaves you guys and the staff. All of us bridesmaids were out at the Salty Dog last night."

"So, you're saying it was one of us guys then?" His irritated tone set her nerves on edge. "Well, it wasn't any of the guys either. We were in a poker game all night."

"Really? And no one left at all? For any reason?"

"It wasn't the guys."

"Well, it wasn't the girls either. Once we got back, Kendra, Georgia, and Beth went to the library, Simone dragged Rachel upstairs, and I went to my room then came to the kitchen to fix myself a cup of tea. That's when I discovered the damage to the cake."

"Why did you need to drag Rachel upstairs?" Mike's question took Haley aback. Was he concerned about her? Maybe her suspicions that Mike and Rachel had had a fling were true. But that had nothing to do with Kendra's wedding, did it?

"She was drunk."

"Oh. Yeah, she can put them away like a guy." Mike pursed his lips. "She can usually hold her own though."

Haley raised a brow but remained silent. Sounded like he knew her pretty well. Haley took a deep breath. It didn't matter how well Mike knew Rachel. She had more important things to worry about.

"Did you have all the lights on when you came into

the kitchen? Did you see anyone or anything out of place when you made your tea?" Mike asked.

"Of course not." She scowled. Who did he think he was? CSI? "It was late, and I didn't want to disturb anybody. I wasn't expecting it to be a crime scene."

"I see." He exhaled slowly. "So basically what you're telling me is you were here, in the dark, snooping around. Did it ever occur to you that maybe the person who damaged the cake was still here too, lurking in the shadows? Hiding so you wouldn't discover them. This is all just getting us nowhere."

"You're right." Haley put her napkin down on the table and stood, doing her best to appear as regal as possible. "I've suddenly lost my appetite. Please excuse me. I've got lots of things to get done today."

With that she walked out, not sparing a single look back at the insufferable Mike Sanderson and his insufferable, inscrutable, incredibly likable face.

"Yikes." Ginny cleared Haley's dishes. "Seems like there's a bit of trouble brewing between the two of you, eh?"

Mike stared down at his hands clasped atop the table and sighed. He'd not meant to goad Haley, and he'd certainly not meant to be rude and chase her off, but his anxieties had gotten the better of him. Besides, after the way she'd run off after kissing him then turned up flirting with the first man she saw, it left Mike feeling decidedly discombobulated. And just who *was* the guy she'd been talking to, anyway?

Of course, the thing with the cake bothered him too. Stabbing a wedding cake wasn't normal behavior no matter how you looked at it. But accusing the gardener didn't sit right with him. He'd meant what he'd said, even if he regretted the bald-faced way he'd said it. It was unlikely the gardener would have a motive to try and stop Kendra and Jared's wedding. After all, she barely knew them. And just because someone was quiet and withdrawn didn't make them a bad person. Maybe Haley should spend less time accusing the gardener and take a good look at the guy she was flirting with.

And the guys *had* all been playing poker all night, hadn't they? Sure, people had gotten up to stretch or use the facilities or whatever, but they'd always come right back, hadn't they?

Honestly, things were a little fuzzy now. He'd had his share of beers, and the late night had become something of a blur.

If what Haley said was true, though, and all the bridesmaids had come either to the library or upstairs, it couldn't be them either. He squeezed his eyes shut and tried to remember the faces he'd seen around the table last night, but again—blurry. That'd teach him not to overindulge. He wasn't a kid anymore.

What bothered him most, though, was the thought of Haley bumping around in that dark kitchen alone with a knife-wielding cake destroyer standing nearby. If the guilty party had panicked and attacked Haley instead...

Mike shuddered. Nope. Not going there. Haley might have made it clear she didn't want him when she'd run out on him, but that didn't mean his protective instincts were gone where she was concerned.

"Are there any other people staying at the inn besides the wedding party and guests?" Mike asked.

Ginny shook her head. "No, why?"

"I saw Haley with a guy I hadn't seen before. I mean, I was just wondering given all the odd goings-on..."

"Well, there are a few people coming and going around here that have a part in the wedding. The caterers have sent people, the minister, the photographer. A few guests have arrived for tonight. Just because they aren't in the wedding party doesn't necessarily mean they don't belong."

So the guy probably was an invited guest. Someone Haley already knew. Someone she had a history with. Someone Mike couldn't compete with.

"True. I guess we'll have to do more detecting before we jump to conclusions." Mike stood as well and kissed Ginny on the cheek. "Thanks for breakfast. It was delicious."

"You're so welcome." Ginny smiled. "Have fun today."

"That's the plan." He headed out onto the back patio, hoping for some time alone to think and relax in the warm sunshine. As he stretched out on a chaise lounge, however, the sound of shears clipping and ground being tilled soon interrupted his peace and quiet. Mike raised his head slightly to peer over the honeysuckle bushes surrounding the patio and see the mysterious gardener that Haley had seemed so suspicious of earlier.

Intent on putting the rumors of her involvement squarely out to pasture, Mike got up and wandered over to where Emery was cultivating a couple of raised flower beds.

"You're Emery, right? The gardener?" He extended his hand and flashed his most charming smile. Well, at least it used to be his most charming. He hadn't used it in a while and wasn't sure it still worked. "Mike Sanderson. I'm here with the wedding party this week."

Apparently the smile no longer worked, because

Emery gave him a wary stare and held tight to the hoe in her grip, ignoring his hand. "Can I help you?"

"Actually, maybe you can. Seems we had a little debacle with the wedding cake last night. Someone apparently got into the walk-in fridge while no one was around and smashed the cake up good. You didn't happen to see anyone around the kitchen last night, say around one or two a.m.? Ginny said you live on-site."

Her dark eyes narrowed, and she took a step back from him. "I do. And no, I didn't see anything. I was up in my room all night."

"What about noises? Maybe someone in the kitchen?"

"No." Her knuckles turned white as she held tight to her implement, and her gaze was averted. Her dark brows knit. "Well, maybe. I thought I heard someone running down the back steps that lead to the kitchen, but I'm not sure what time that was. Shortly after the girls came back."

"Right. Okay." He didn't know her well enough to say whether or not she was lying to him, but given her defensive posture and her lack of eye contact, it seemed like she definitely had something to hide. Emery's eyes flickered to the scars on his arm before gazing out to sea. Or maybe she just couldn't stand the sight of him. That seemed to be catching these days.

"Hey, bud," Jared called from his second-floor window. "Bunch of us are going to head down to the beach again soon. You want to come with?"

"Sure," Mike yelled back then turned to find Emery working on her flowers again. "Thanks for talking to me."

She glanced back at him over her shoulder. "Be careful on those stairs. I've seen your group using them a couple of times already. They're rotted out in some spots. Ginny hasn't had the money to fix them yet, and it's a long fall down to the bottom of the cliffs."

Taken by surprise, Mike nodded and backed toward the inn again. There was a vague threat lodged somewhere in her warning that set all his instincts on high alert. Still, if she was involved in the mishaps around here, he didn't want to tip Emery off that he was on to her. He waved and forced a polite smile as he turned and walked away.

CHAPTER SIXTEEN

*H*aley followed the rest of the wedding party over to the top of the stairs at the cliff's edge. Everyone seemed to still be recovering from their bout of drinking the night before. Everyone except Rachel, that was. Maybe she recovered quickly or had a secret hangover remedy. That might account for her incessant cheerfulness this morning. Or maybe the woman was just terminally annoying.

Given the debacle with the wedding cake the night before and the hassle poor Ginny had gone through this morning to get a new one ordered in time for the reception tonight, Haley was going with the second option. She was so *not* in the mood for cheerful this morning.

Up ahead, Rachel clung to Kendra's arm, chattering

away like they weren't all suffering from pounding heads. Kendra, for her part, looked to be tolerating her friend's nonstop talking with the patience of a saint.

"Enough with the chatter, Rach." Simone put her hand on her head. "Let us recover a bit first."

She looped her arm through Kendra's other arm. "The bride needs her beauty silence. Right, Ken?"

"I'm sure we'll all be much more chipper after a dip," Kendra said.

Simone led them over to the top of the stairs. Only two at a time could fit, and Rachel stepped aside then made a sweeping gesture and a slight bow toward Kendra. "Brides first."

Waves gently rolled toward the shore, and the sun shone bright in the clear blue sky, and everything seemed about as wonderful as anyone could ask for on their wedding day. The group made their way slowly down the rickety old stairs toward the beach below, talking and laughing. The guys were making jokes about how many pennies they'd lost in their poker game the night before.

It was all enough to lull Haley into a pleasant daze.

CRRACCCCKKKK!!!

The loud sound ripped through the air, followed by screams and people scrambling. Haley clasped tight to the wooden railing beside her as she reached out to grab her sister around the waist to keep her from tumbling down the steep stairs.

About five feet ahead, splintered wood dangled free in the air from the shattered railing.

"Oh my God!" Kendra said, clinging tight to Haley's arm. "The railing broke!"

Rachel was crouched on the steps, gripping the edge of the one she was sitting on with white knuckles. "Is everyone all right?"

Shouts and murmurs rippled through the crowd as Jared pushed his way down the precarious stairs to check on Kendra. Mike followed right behind him, his gaze locked on Haley the entire time.

"What happened?" Mike asked as Jared comforted a shaken Kendra.

"The railing broke," Haley said, her voice shaking as badly as her knees. For once she envied her sister having someone to comfort her in her time of need. Mike stood with his hands on his hips, his biceps rippling in the sunshine.

For a moment, she imagined how wonderful it would feel to have those strong arms around her, protecting her like Jared was protecting her sister. But she quickly shoved those thoughts aside. Mike had made it clear he wasn't really interested in her that way, and she needed to move on. "I'm not sure how it happened. It looks pretty old though."

Mike sidled over to take a look at the damage, scowling. "The staff told me Ginny hasn't had time to have them repaired yet. Maybe we should go back up top and take the car down to the beach."

"No," Kendra said, lifting her head from where she'd buried it against her soon-to-be-husband's chest. "We're halfway down already. Let's just finish this so we can all relax before the ceremony. We'll just be more careful."

The rest of the party carefully made their way down to the bottom of the stairs, leaving only Mike and Haley behind. She did her best to avoid his gaze and instead stared at the busted railing. "Do you think someone did this on purpose?"

"Not sure." He crouched again to study the underside of the wood, and Haley did her best not to stare at how the khaki cotton of his swim trunks stretched tight across his muscled thighs and butt. He pointed at the wood, and she forced her attention away from his sleek body. "This doesn't look like it rotted out though. I mean, there is some rot, but the break is clean, suggesting it wasn't natural causes."

"Great." Haley sighed and rolled her stiff neck. "More to worry about today."

"C'mon." He surprised her by taking her hand and

leading her down the steps, carefully scanning each step to make sure it wasn't rotted through or tampered with. "Let's catch up with the others."

At the bottom, she was grateful for the feel of the warm sand squishing through her icy toes as she and Mike walked over to where the rest of the group was setting up. Most had brought towels, though a few had chairs, and Rachel even managed to somehow squeeze a beach umbrella in that seemingly bottomless tote of hers. And the guys, of course, had lugged the cooler along. Wouldn't be a day at the beach without libations, she supposed.

As soon as they were in sight of the others, Mike let go of Haley's hand and walked on ahead to toss his towel down beside the rest of the guys' stuff. She missed the heat of his touch almost immediately, but she refused to let him see that he affected her that much. Instead, she concentrated on setting up her own towel on the ground beside Rachel. She would've preferred to sit next to Kendra, but her sister was the center of attention that day, and all those spots were already occupied.

They spent the next hour or so chatting and reading or snoozing, the coconut smell of sunscreen spicing the air. The guys splashed around in the water while the girls sunbathed. Haley was glad for time to catch up on her to-be-read pile. Not much time for that back home in

Nebraska, with students to attend to and classes to plan. She placed a hand atop her head to keep her hat in place as a gust of wind drifted in off the ocean, carrying with it the sting of warm sand and salt.

The side of her neck tingled, as if someone was staring at her. Haley shifted around to glance up at the cliff top where the inn was located and spotted Emery, the gardener, staring down at them again—just like she'd been watching them from the beach that day of the bee attack.

Haley wasn't ready to rule her out yet. Yes, Mike was right in saying a motive was difficult to establish, but not impossible. After all, crazy didn't really need a reason to act out, did it?

Perhaps this Emery had some secret agenda when it came to the inn. Ginny had said she'd just started and was a bit secretive. Maybe she wanted to somehow hurt Ginny's business, and what better way to do that than bad publicity from a guest being injured on the premises?

The more she thought about it, the more it made sense. Emery couldn't have known Kendra would be the one to nearly fall, but then, if the gardener had never had a specific target to begin with, it wouldn't have mattered. Harming the inn's reputation only required that *someone* fall.

New ideas percolating, Haley made a mental note to talk to Jared on the way back to the inn and warn him to make sure that Kendra was well protected until the wedding was over and they'd left for their honeymoon. If Emery wanted to mess with the inn's reputation, let her do it at someone else's event.

CHAPTER SEVENTEEN

*L*ater, Haley was helping Kendra get ready for the wedding ceremony in Kendra's room. Her sister had snagged her on the way back from the beach—right after Haley and Jared had agreed that between the two of them they would keep an eye on Kendra. If it was Emery, she might be targeting *anyone*, but Haley was most concerned that the day not be ruined for Kendra.

Kendra had wanted to spend some time with Haley getting prettied up before the ceremony. She'd said it would be just like when they were growing up. Given the cramped nature of the space and Kendra's frenetic prewedding energy, Haley wasn't so sure, but she'd gone along with it anyway. It would give her a chance to keep an eye on her sister.

Haley finished putting another coat of polish on her toenails then set the bottle aside while Kendra worked on curling her hair in the mirror.

"So?" Her sister's smile was devious, and her eyes twinkled. "What's up with you and Mike?"

"Nothing." Haley frowned. "Why?"

"Didn't look like nothing. I saw the way he was holding your hand on the way down to the beach."

"Jeez. What are we? In fourth grade or something?" Haley scoffed and shook her head. "There's nothing between Mike and me. He was helping me down the stairs so I didn't fall."

"I'm sure he was." Kendra winked into the mirror. "He's super handsome and such a nice guy. I don't blame you at all for testing those waters."

"I'm not testing anything." Haley feigned renewed interest in her freshly painted toes, wriggling them so the bright-pink color showed iridescent in the late-afternoon sun. "Besides, I've been told he's nothing but a player. Only looking for another notch in his bedpost."

"Seriously?" This time it was Kendra's turn to scoff. "I don't know what you're talking about."

"Come on. A guy that good-looking must have women crawling all over him." She sat back and crossed her arms, leaning against the wall behind the bed. "No way would he even look twice at some small-town teacher from Nebraska."

"Listen." Kendra unplugged her curler and set it aside to cool before joining her sister on the bed. "I don't know who you've been talking to about Mike Sanderson, but you've been severely misinformed. He hasn't dated anyone since he and Jared were discharged from Special Ops."

"Really?" Haley's heart leapt with a mix of surprise and hope before she could stop it.

"Really." Kendra grabbed her pillow and held it in her lap, tight ringlets dangling around her face. "Jared said Mike had a girlfriend—Courtney, I think her name was—but she dumped him after he got out of the hospital. Said she couldn't deal with all his grueling rehab and that she didn't want to be saddled with a guy who was scarred like him."

Chest squeezing with sorrow for Mike, Haley blinked back the unexpected sting of tears. How could anyone turn their back on such a smart, generous, kind, and gentle man? Especially when he needed them most? The thought of Mike alone during his darkest hours broke Haley's heart.

"Actually, it was Jared who was the player." Kendra gave a sad little snort. "He was a serial womanizer for a while after he and Mike returned Stateside. But that was because he was in such a bad place after the trial and discharge. Thank God, he had Mike to help him through it. That's why they're so close. Well, that and whatever happened over in the Middle East that led to their discharge. Jared still won't tell me about it. He said it was in the past, and he wanted it to stay there."

She didn't like the idea of her sister's fiancé keeping secrets, but the sooner she remembered Kendra was an adult and could make her own choices, the better. Haley was an adult too, and she'd spent so much time being invested in the notion that Mike was nothing but a playboy only looking for a good time and that he'd never be interested in a woman like her that it was hard to make a complete one-eighty so fast.

"Who told you all that stuff about Mike anyway?"

"Rachel." Haley shrugged. "She said both Mike and Jared were party animals where women were concerned."

"Hmm." Kendra shook her head and shrugged. "Well, I suppose she would feel that way. Jared used to date some of the girls in the group. Nothing too serious from what he said." Kendra shrugged. "That's all in the past, too."

"Interesting." Haley picked at the lace border on the quilted duvet and scrunched her nose. It wasn't Mike Rachel had been talking about when she'd made the comment about notches in his belt, it was Jared. So, maybe all those times Mike had been nice to her, talked to her, kissed her, he hadn't been playing her. Maybe he'd really liked her. Then he'd stopped, apparently. At least if his current cold attitude toward her was any indication. "He kissed me."

"Who?" Kendra frowned. "Jared?"

"No, silly. Mike. In the gardens one day while I was scoping out locations for the photographer."

"Oh my God, sis! That's awesome! How was it?"

Heat flooded Haley's cheeks as she remembered the heart-stopping kiss they'd shared.

"That good, huh?" Kendra waggled her brows.

"Yeah. Great, actually." Haley couldn't suppress her smile. "But he doesn't want anything to do with me now. He's been giving me the brush-off since."

"Huh. That doesn't sound like Mike." Kendra tapped her finger on her lips, her expression thoughtful. "What happened after the kiss?"

"I had to run off to an appointment. Then I got busy. I had to meet with the photographer and talk to Stacy and Ginny about some things for the reception, but that was about it."

Realization dawned in her sister's gaze. "Did Mike see you talking to the photographer?"

"Maybe. It was on the side of the house, so I guess he probably did. Why?"

"Did you tell him that's who you were meeting?"

Haley thought back. Truth was, she wasn't sure what she'd said. She'd been all flummoxed with the kiss, and then the clock chimed and she didn't want to be late. "I'm not sure."

Kendra gave a curt nod. "Is the photographer young, old, good-looking?"

"Well, he's about our age, I suppose." Haley frowned. "I didn't really notice his looks, but I suppose he's okay, if you like that bookish, nerdy type."

"Right." Kendra nudged her sister's leg and grinned. "Let's think about this from Mike's perspective. He kissed you. It was amazing. Then you suddenly leave right afterward to go talk to another guy. Is it possible he thought you were giving *him* the brush-off?"

Haley hadn't considered the situation from that angle before. Could it be all the weirdness between her and Mike now was her fault and not his? "Maybe."

"I know it sounds far-fetched, but you need to understand Mike's still really self-conscious about his burn scars. Jared's said he's got it in his head that since his girlfriend left him, no woman's going to want him anymore. Crazy but true."

CHAPTER EIGHTEEN

*W*hile the women were upstairs, doing whatever it was they did on their wedding day, Mike and Jared were chilling out on the patio behind the inn, just below Kendra's window. They'd both showered and shaved, which took all of about twenty minutes. Now, with two hours left until the big ceremony, there wasn't much for them to do. Jared had chosen their spot because he'd said he wanted to stay nearby in case Kendra needed him. Mike had seen Haley talking to Jared when they'd left the beach earlier, so maybe she'd warned him about the sabotage and the crazy cake destroyer on the loose.

Jared gave Mike a sideways glance then leaned back in his chair to take a swig from his bottled water. "What's up with you and Haley?"

"Nothing." Mike frowned and stared down at the pebble he was nudging with his toe. "Why?"

"Didn't look like nothing to me." Jared shrugged. "Not that it's any of my business, man. But she's Kendra's sister, you know? I don't want you screwing up my wedding night for me."

"Whatever." Mike kicked the pebble away then stared out over the gardens. Hard to believe that a day earlier, he and Haley had been kissing in there. Now she'd already moved on to someone else. And yeah, he was angry. More at himself than anyone. He'd been such an idiot, thinking she was different than every other woman he'd met since his injuries and discharge. They'd all taken one look at his scars and run the other way as fast as their legs would carry them. He shook his head and cracked open the lid of his own bottle of water.

Not that he could blame them. He was damaged goods now. Simple as that.

Jared squinted one eye closed as he stared at Mike. "Aw, damn. You like her, don't you?"

"What? No." Truth was, Mike more than liked Haley. In fact, if he allowed himself to go down that path, thinking she might be his, he saw a total future with her—marriage, house, family, the whole nine yards. Not that he wanted to tell Jared that. Discussing his feelings with his buddies was *not* something he was comfortable with, no matter how close they were. "I've just been trying to be nice to her. That's all. It's what you asked me to do, right?"

"Yeah." Jared crossed his arms, not looking convinced at all. "Saw you holding her hand today on the beach."

"I was helping her down the steps."

"You stare at her every time she's in the room."

"So?"

"So, I've known you long enough to know when you're into someone."

"Why are we even talking about this, dude?" Mike looked away, heat pulsating from his cheeks and his blood pounding in his ears. God, had his attraction to Haley been that obvious? He'd been out of the game for a while now, but he'd not thought he'd lost his touch that much. "Forget about it, okay? There's nothing between Haley and me now."

Jared raised a dark brow. "But there was?"

"Seriously?" Mike said, exasperated. "Since when are you so nosy? You're worse than a woman."

"Since my soon-to-be wife started hounding me about fixing you up with someone nice." Jared exhaled slowly and scrubbed a hand through his short, dark-brown hair. "She's got it in her head that Haley likes you, and she thinks the two of you would be good together. I tried to talk Kendra out of it, but you know how she gets when there's matchmaking involved. Remember how she was when she set up those two radiology techs at the hospital?"

Haley likes me? He stopped listening after those words. For a moment, Mike didn't know how to answer. He liked her too. A lot. More than was wise, probably. But none of it mattered now since she obviously preferred that guy he'd seen her talking to near the side of the house after she'd fled from their kiss in the garden.

Mike looked up and saw Jared still watching him. *Damn.* The guy was like a dog with a bone. He wouldn't let this go until Mike gave him something. "Well, it doesn't matter what Haley feels about me now. She's got a boyfriend."

"She does?" Jared scrunched his nose. "Since when?"

"Since yesterday morning. Saw her talking to the guy myself."

"Well, that's news to Kendra, then, because she doesn't know anything about a boyfriend."

For the first time, a niggle of doubt crept into Mike's thoughts. Could it be the conversation he'd seen between Haley and that mystery guy wasn't as flirtatious as it looked? Had he let his own doubts and insecurities misread the situation? He sighed and slumped in his chair. Now that he really thought about it rationally, it was entirely possible. What with his investigation into who might be trying to ruin the wedding and his swirling feelings about Haley after that scorching kiss, he hadn't exactly been thinking with the clearest head.

There was a clatter of equipment from somewhere out in the gardens, followed by a low curse. Both Jared and Mike immediately straightened, searching for the source of the noise. Jared must've spotted the culprit first, because he visibly relaxed and chuckled. "Just the wedding photographer."

He pointed toward a guy crouched near a pile of equipment near a copse of rosebushes. Mike glanced over then did a double take. It was the same guy Haley had been talking to near the side of the house after their kiss. He thought back to their conversation that morning as they'd strolled the gardens, and he remembered her saying something about meeting with the photographer.

Well, crap. He started laughing.

Jared gave him an odd look. "What's so funny?"

"I'm an idiot."

"Well, yeah. That's nothing new."

"There you guys are," Rachel said, carrying out a silver tray of tiny sandwiches, preempting Mike's smartass retort. "The cook asked me to bring these out to you.

She said you need some sustenance to get you through the big ceremony. Dinner isn't until six thirty."

Mike passed. He was too focused on how badly he might've screwed up things between him and Haley to be hungry. Jared, however, readily accepted two of the sandwiches, devouring them in about three bites each. The guy had always been ravenous when it came to food. Mike never could figure out where he put it all, because he never put on an ounce of extra weight.

"How do they taste?" Rachel asked, watching as Jared grabbed a third sandwich and shoved it in his mouth. From what Mike could tell, they were some frou-frou kind—watercress or maybe cucumber, based on the odd greenish color of the crap inside. Either way, he wasn't touching that stuff.

"Fine," Jared said, finishing off his last bite then standing. He stretched then slid his sunglasses back into place. "Are Kendra and Haley still up in their room getting ready?"

"As far as I know," Rachel said. "You can't go up there though. Bad luck to see the bride before the ceremony."

"Don't worry." Jared started back into the inn with Mike by his side. "I'm just going to talk to her through the door. No peeking. Kendra already read me the riot act about seeing her in her dress. See you in a couple of hours."

Mike waved to Rachel then followed Jared to the inn in search of Haley. If he was lucky, he could catch her before the ceremony and try to put things right between them. And if he wasn't lucky, well... then it was going to be a very long night.

CHAPTER NINETEEN

*H*aley finished fussing with her hair and makeup then stared at her reflection in the mirror. She'd taken her time showering, secure that Kendra was locked in her room. She thought she might have heard someone knocking on her door while she was in the shower, but she didn't want to talk to anyone. She needed to focus on getting ready so she'd have extra time to help Kendra and make sure she didn't spend one minute alone where she might be in danger.

She sat at the dressing table and tamed her riotous coppery curls atop her head for the wedding, with a few tendrils curling down around her face. A flowered headband with crystals was secured near the crown. All the bridesmaids were wearing one to match the larger, more ornate one Kendra would have in her hair to hold her veil. The ebony mascara on her naturally thick lashes, atop sparkling pink shadow, was way more than she usually wore, but even she had to admit they brought out her hazel eyes and made her look almost like a wide-eyed Disney fairy princess.

Now all she had to do was get into her dress and she'd be ready.

She walked out of her attached bath and stared at the lace-and-satin blush-pink formal dress laid out atop her bed. It was a great color, good on just about every skin tone, and once more Haley had to applaud her sister's choices, both in clothes and in men. Turned out Jared was a good guy after all. Mike too, if what Kendra had told her about him was true.

A glance at her clock showed she still had half an hour before she was scheduled to meet the rest of the bridesmaids in Kendra's room to go down to the ceremony together. She wasn't exactly keen on squeezing into the uncomfortable outfit and stiletto pumps that went along with it just yet, so she opted for slipping into a comfy pair of cutoff shorts and a tank top for the time being. Besides, she didn't want to wrinkle her pretty dress by sitting in it either. She slid her feet into her flip-flops then walked over to the window seat, staring out at the ocean beyond.

Maybe she did still have a chance with Mike. Yes,

she'd screwed up, but if she was honest, she really liked him, more than she had anyone else in a long, long time. And yes, the distance between them back home might be an issue, but not insurmountable, if they were both willing to compromise.

Darn. She should've asked Kendra how Mike might feel about that—how married he was to his job in Sioux Falls—when they'd talked earlier. Perhaps it wasn't too late to ask her now. She could always talk to Mike directly, but after the way she messed things up between them, she needed the extra confidence boost that Kendra's enthusiasm for her and Mike to start a relationship would give her.

She walked out into the hall to her sister's door.

"Hey, kiddo. Can I come in for a second?" She knocked softly on Kendra's door.

No answer.

Haley tried again. "Kendra? I just have a quick question for you."

Still nothing.

Growing concerned, she tried the door handle and found it unlocked. Weird, because she and Jared had both made Kendra promise to lock the door if she was in the room, and she always locked the door when she wasn't in.

But where would she have gone? Somewhere with

Jared? Haley doubted that. Maybe Kendra had forgotten to lock the door in the prewedding excitement and was in the bathroom getting ready and had her ear buds in. If her music was loud, she wouldn't hear anything at all. Haley creaked the door open then stopped abruptly, her heart skidding.

Jared was sprawled on the floor, not moving, his face pale. Worse, there was no sign of Kendra at all.

Panicked, Haley rushed in and checked Jared's pulse. Steady, but he didn't wake up, no matter how hard she shook him. Knees shaking, Haley whipped her head around, checking the room. Kendra's wedding dress was still draped over the bed. Her shoes on the floor. Her makeup out, curling iron on the dresser. She darted into the bathroom but found no sign of her sister. Maybe she'd gone to get help for Jared?

A moan issued from behind her, and she rushed back to Jared's side.

"Hey," Haley said, patting his cheek. "Jared, can you tell me what happened? Where's my sister?"

He blinked open groggy eyes, a deep frown creasing his brow. "G-gone."

His words slurred as if he'd been drugged. "Where is she, Jared? What do you mean gone?"

"Scheee took her..." he managed to get out before passing out again.

Mind racing and heart thudding hard against her ribs, Haley stood and backed away. Someone *took* her?

Jared was passed out and Kendra was gone, and she had no idea how to find her baby sister. Why hadn't she trusted her gut? Why hadn't she taken the sabotage against this wedding more seriously? Why would anyone want to hurt Kendra? Why?

She rushed into the hallway. "Help! Something's happened to Jared and Kendra! Help!"

The hallway erupted with doors opening and people rushing out in various states of undress.

"What happened?" Georgia looked at her with concerned eyes as everyone congregated pulling on T-shirts and cinching robes.

Haley pointed to Kendra's room. "In there! Something happened to Jared, and Kendra is missing."

"Missing?" Georgia looked around as Todd, Mark, and Beth rushed into Kendra's room. "Maybe she's just downstairs."

Haley shook her head, turning back toward Kendra's room, where Todd was kneeling beside Jared. "He said someone took her."

In the room, Todd lifted one of Jared's eyelids then slapped his cheek gently. "Jared, buddy, can you hear me?"

Jared shook his head slightly, his eyes flickered open

for a second, and he mumbled something unintelligible, then his eyes snapped shut.

"He's out cold," Todd said. "Looks like he was drugged."

Drugged? Someone had drugged Jared and taken Kendra, and Haley wasn't going to find her by hanging out in this room. She rushed out the door, wishing Mike was with her. He hadn't come out of his room when she yelled, but he might have been in the shower or maybe he was outside. Either way, she didn't have time to find him. Precious seconds were being wasted that could put Kendra in deeper danger.

She raced downstairs, almost smashing into Rachel halfway down.

Rachel put her hands on Haley's shoulders to steady her. "What's going on? I heard yelling."

"Someone drugged Jared and took Kendra."

"What? That's crazy. Who would do that?"

Haley pushed away. Taking the steps two at a time, she shot over her shoulder, "I have no idea, but I have to find her."

"Oh, so it must have been you that sent Simone out into the garden to look for her. That's why she was running."

Haley stopped short, her mind whirling. Simone? Wait, she hadn't been one of the people out in the hallway or in Kendra's room. How would she have known to go look for Kendra? Haley looked up the stairs at Rachel. "Simone was running in the garden?"

Rachel frowned. "Yeah, she was headed toward the back where that shed is. I thought it was weird, but..."

Haley didn't stop to listen to the rest of her chatter. She turned and bolted down the stairs, passing Ginny and yelling for her to call the police. She burst out the conservatory door and into the gardens.

How could she have been so stupid? Of course, it had been Simone the whole time. Simone had been around when Kendra's suitcase broke, and she could have easily taken all those items that had gone missing as well as messed with the lanterns.

At the bachelorette party in the bar when Rachel had made that remark about how Jared and Mike played around and not being another notch, she'd used the word "we," and the only other person there had been Simone. Haley had assumed it was Rachel that didn't want to be another notch on Mike's belt, but what if it was Simone and Jared that had had the affair? Hadn't Kendra suggested that Jared had a thing going with one of the girls in the wedding party before he met her? What if that girl was Simone, and Simone had never really gotten over Jared?

When they'd returned home from the bachelorette

party, Simone had escorted the drunken Rachel to her room down at the end of the hall, where the back stairs that led to the kitchen were. She could have easily dropped Rachel into bed and run down the stairs into the kitchen. Whoever took Kendra would have had to be strong to wrestle her out—maybe they'd drugged her or knocked her out, but Kendra wouldn't go on her own. But that night, Simone had said she could carry Rachel if she had to, because she was used to it with her nursing work.

And hadn't Mike said that *Simone* asked him if he wanted a peanut butter, honey, and banana sandwich that morning on the beach? And as he'd pointed out, anyone could Google how to cut power to a house and bring a pair of insulated wire cutters with them on the trip. And how hard would it be to cut the stairway railing? An image of Simone standing arm in arm with Kendra at the entrance to the rickety stairs that morning bubbled up. She'd practically led Kendra down there first. She must have been planning this for a long time.

Haley's stomach plummeted as she raced into the gardens. The longer Kendra was missing, the less chance there was of finding her alive. She'd watched enough true-crime shows on TV to know the first forty-eight hours were the most crucial in any missing-persons case.

"Kendra! Simone! Where are you?" she yelled as she

raced toward the back of the garden, pushing branches aside and swatting at overgrown shrubs on her way to the shed.

Her heart leapt when the shed came into view. The door was partially open, and she thought she saw movement inside. She slowed a bit, not sure if she should give herself away. She might need the element of surprise if Simone was holding Kendra hostage.

She crept up to the door, her heart thudding against her rib cage. In the dimmer interior light, she squinted to see the silhouette of two figures in the corner—one on the ground, tied up and squirming and one standing over the tied-up figure as if ready to strike.

Beside the open door was an old wooden shovel. In one swift movement, Haley leapt through the doorway, grabbed the shovel, and held it overhead.

"Touch her and I swear you'll regret it."

Simone spun around, and Haley's heart jumped, her brows mashed together in confusion.

The kidnapper wasn't Simone... it was Emery.

CHAPTER TWENTY

"*I*t was you all along!" Haley tightened her grip on the shovel.

"What are you talking about?" Emery must have been totally nuts, because she looked genuinely perplexed. Haley snuck a glance at Kendra, who was squirming with the ropes. Relief flooded through her upon seeing her sister wasn't too badly harmed.

Haley glanced at the rows of tools that hung on the wall. Were any of those insulated wire cutters? And were those jars of honey lined up on the workbench? Haley remembered Emery peeking down at them on the beach the day of the bee incident. Ginny had said Emery took care of the beehives—had she done something to make the bees swarm? There had only been one bee, but maybe whatever she'd done hadn't worked as well as she'd thought it would.

Emery had warned them about the steps—probably to deflect suspicion in case anyone realized the railing had been tampered with, most likely with one of the many saws hanging on the wall across from her. Come to think of it, Emery was one of the few people who had been in the inn but unaccounted for when the cake had been ruined. But *why* would Emery be doing this?

"Why are you doing this? What do you want with my sister?" Haley stepped closer, the shovel still overhead. In Emery's delusional state, she was apt to do anything. Haley would have to be cautious if she wanted to overpower her.

"I don't want anything from your sister," Emery said. "Except to get her out of my shed. I don't know what kind of weird games you people are up to, but I'd appreciate it if you'd help me with her."

"Why did you tie Kendra up and hide her out here?"

"I didn't." Emery held up her hands in surrender when Haley waved the shovel menacingly. "I swear. I came out here to get one of my tools, and I found her like this. Help me untie her so I can get back to my work."

Unsure, Haley hesitated. "I don't—"

She never got to finish that sentence. Someone shoved her hard in the back, and the shovel clattered to the ground as she tripped headlong into Emery. They ended up in a pile atop Kendra on the floor. Through the dim light and the hair that had tumbled into her face, Haley looked at the figure in the doorway.

Rachel.

Rachel's lips turned up in a sneer as she looked in at them. "Lucky me. I can play the hero today and finally make Jared fall in love with me, just like he should have all along. He's mine! Not yours, Kendra. I thought you were my friend, but you only hung around me to steal Jared away, didn't you?"

Kendra groaned and mumbled around the gag in her mouth. Haley scrambled off of her sister and Emery to try and reach Rachel.

Haley's head spun with the sickening realization that Rachel had tricked her. She should have followed her gut instincts; she hadn't liked Rachel from the beginning.

Now it made perfect sense. Images of the sticky bag from Rachel's peanut-butter-and-honey sandwich sitting on the blanket in between Rachel and Kendra came to mind. The bee had landed on Mike's sandwich, but Rachel had probably intended for it to land near Kendra.

No wonder she hadn't seemed hungover this morning. She must have been faking being so drunk at the pub and run down to the kitchen as soon as Simone dropped her off in her room. Being passed out was a perfect alibi.

When she'd mentioned not being another notch on someone's belt, it was *Jared* she was talking about. Rachel was the one Jared had had a fling with, and apparently she'd never gotten over it.

"Why are you doing this?" Haley moved slowly, keeping her voice deliberately calm. "Please, just let us go, and no one needs to know about this."

"No. It's too late." Rachel glanced over her shoulder then back at Haley. "My plan has already been put in motion. Too bad you were so jealous of your sister that you tried to kill her, Haley."

"What are you talking about?" Haley took a step closer, Emery right behind her. How long would it take before others came here from the inn? Or would they? Rachel might have gone right up to Kendra's room after she met Haley on the stairs and pointed them in another direction.

"Oh, you know why. You didn't want Kendra to get married, did you? The thought of losing her made you crazy. So you had to kill her."

"What? No one will believe that," Haley said while Kendra wriggled and kicked out.

Rachel's grin sent a shiver up Haley's spine. "Already set the stage. I told Simone that you confessed to me that you didn't know what you were going to do now that Kendra had Jared. I even said you seemed a little crazed. Later tonight, after I'm discovered as the hero, it will come out that you drugged Jared and Simone so that you could take Kendra away. At least that's what everyone is going to deduce when I tell them that you gave me the sandwiches with express instructions to make sure only Jared and Simone ate certain ones... Too bad none of you will be around to refute my story."

So that was why Simone had not been in the hall with the others. She was already drugged in her room. Rachel had drugged Jared and taken Kendra. She and Simone had said they could lift anyone because of their nursing training. Then she'd come back to the inn and been lurking around downstairs, just waiting for Haley to discover that Kendra was missing so she could send her out into the gardens and get her into the shed too. But what about Emery? Haley glanced at the gardener.

"Yeah, too bad. Looks like Emery will be collateral damage." Rachel shrugged.

The shed was deep in the garden, hidden by foliage and trees. If Rachel had spun some tale back at the inn about seeing them take off in the other direction, it could be days before anyone thought to look here.

"Oh well. Toodles. This is my last chance to get Jared back before the wedding. I'm sorry, but I love him too much to let him go."

With that, she slammed the shed door closed and slid the lock into place.

Even through the stench of dirt and fertilizer, the sharp smell of gasoline permeated the air. In the pitch blackness, Haley fumbled her way back to where she thought Emery and Kendra were. Her eyes hadn't adjusted yet, and it was hard to see. She felt an arm, then huddled near them again.

Together, she and Emery managed to get Kendra free.

"How are we going to get out of here?" her sister asked, voice cracked and dry from the gag.

"No idea," Haley said, her words severed by a heart-stopping *scritch* followed by an unmistakable crackle. "Oh, God. Is that what I think it is?"

Emery's tone held the shrill sharpness of terror. "Fire!"

CHAPTER TWENTY-ONE

ike knelt beside Jared, his gut knotting as he shook Jared hard again. "Wake up, dammit! Kendra's missing. She's in trouble. She needs you!"

Jared mumbled something incoherent, his eyes rolling back in his head again.

"Looks like he's been given some sort of benzodiazepine. Maybe Valium or diazepam. It needs to wear off, but I think he'll be okay," Todd said. Mike was grateful that Jared had a bunch of doctors around in the wedding party.

But even though Jared would be fine, there was no way his buddy could save the day, not this time, but Mike damned sure could. He would, too, because he owed Jared his life. Time to repay that debt.

He climbed to his feet and raced out of Kendra's room into the chaos in the hallway. All the bridesmaids were there, as was Ginny. Everyone was buzzing about Kendra. But wait, where was Haley?

She hadn't answered when he'd knocked on her door earlier. What if whoever had taken Kendra had also taken Haley? Both of them could be in trouble, and he wasn't about to wait around for the cops to come to find them.

He bounded down the steps toward the kitchen, almost barreling over Rachel at the bottom of the stairs. He grabbed her shoulders to steady her. "Have you seen Haley?"

"What's going on? Why are you running?" Rachel asked, wide-eyed.

"You haven't heard?"

"Heard what? I was napping out on one of the lawn chairs. Gotta sleep off my hangover before tonight." She peered over his shoulder up the stairs. "Sounds like chaos up there. Did something happen?"

Impatient to get going, Mike explained quickly, "Someone drugged Jared and took Kendra. Haley is missing too."

Rachel frowned. "Missing? Huh. I thought I saw them down on that jetty on the beach about a half hour ago. I had pulled the lawn chair close to the cliffs for the view and so no one would wake me up. I didn't go down though. Looked like they were arguing."

Rachel started up the stairs. "I better go see if Jared's okay. He might need me."

Right. Whatever. Mike was already halfway on his way to the rickety steps that led to the beach. He stopped at the top and scanned the area below. Rachel had said she'd seen them near the rocks, but he didn't see anyone. His stomach sank. The beach was empty.

Maybe she'd been further down... where was that lawn chair? But Mike's frantic search didn't find any lawn chair, and no one appeared on the beach. The more he looked, the more that ominous feeling in the pit of his stomach grew.

It wasn't like Haley and Kendra to argue, and Rachel never got hungover. Plus he'd gotten a weird vibe from Rachel on the stairs. Not to mention the predatory gleam in her eye when she had headed up to make sure Jared was okay. Had she said something about Jared *needing* her? She was Kendra's best friend, so shouldn't she have been more concerned about Kendra? She had had that fling with Jared before he met Kendra, but Mike had thought that didn't mean anything. At least it hadn't to Jared.

Todd had said that someone gave Jared Valium or diazepam. Rachel would have access to that. What if...

Mike turned back toward the house. He needed to ask Rachel more questions. From his vantage point, he could see to the back of the garden, and what he saw there froze his blood. Wisps of smoke coming from the exact area where that toolshed was. It was on *fire.*

Cold terror trickled down his spine, and he was immediately back in that Afghan village, passing out care packages and candy to the local kids. They'd all been so happy, clustered around him to get their share, laughing and giggling as he tried to talk to them in broken Arabic. And yeah, sure, maybe he and Jared weren't technically supposed to be there that day, but they'd figured no one would notice if a couple of grunts went AWOL for a few hours. It was worth it to see those poor kids smile for a change.

Then came the ominous whistle of an incoming missile.

There hadn't been time to get out, time to duck, time to do anything but throw himself atop the kids closest to him to save their lives. The concussive force of the explosion must've knocked him out for a second, because when he came to, all he could hear were the plaintive cries for help from the injured, the acrid stench of smoke filling his nose and choking his lungs. The horrified look on Jared's face as he'd pulled Mike from the smoldering wreckage of the destroyed school building and seen the burns on his neck and arm for the first time.

Mike had blacked out after that, thankfully. The next time he'd woken up, he'd been in the Army hospital, doped up on narcotics and being read the charges against him by the same MPs who would later testify at his and Jared's discharge trial.

He sprinted toward the back of the house and the gardens. It was like a maze trying to find anything in there, but at last he spotted a rusted tin roof through the shrubs and trees. As he neared, his heart dropped to his toes. Thick black smoke filled the air, and flames licked up the sides of the small whitewashed utility building.

His gut churned, his instincts screaming at him to run in the other direction. But then he thought of Haley. She could be inside. He charged for the shed.

Frantic screams echoed from inside and halted him in his tracks. Images of the burning school meshed with the flaming shed, and it took all he had to shake off the paralyzing memories and rush to the metal door of the building. The handle was too hot to touch, so he peeled off his polo shirt and wrapped it around his hand, banging on the rusted bolt jammed into the lock until it came free.

Coughing and squinting, he peered through the

smoke inside, searching for any signs of life. "Haley? Are you in there?"

"Mike?"

Before he could even answer, Haley launched herself into his arms, Kendra and—Mike was surprised to see—Emery right behind her. The four of them stumbled up the path, away from the shed, before the girls collapsed on the ground, coughing and sputtering.

"Ra... chel." Kendra coughed out the name.

"She shut you in there?" Mike glanced at Emery, who had jumped to her feet and then immediately doubled over in a coughing fit, her hands braced on her knees. What did the gardener have to do with all of this?

"There's no time to explain," Haley said. "We have to stop her. She's unstable!"

But before they could do anything, the path behind them exploded with the sound of pounding footsteps. Mike turned to see the other groomsmen running, with Todd in the front, carrying a fire extinguisher that he must have grabbed from the kitchen. The bridesmaids were only a few steps behind them.

"We saw the flames from the house!" Mark yelled, then stopped short when he saw Haley and Kendra. "Haley, Kendra... you're here. But Rachel said..."

They all turned to look at Rachel. Her eyes were

crazed as they darted from one member of the group to the other. "But I saw them, I—"

"Liar! You tied me up!" Kendra said.

Something flickered in Rachel's eyes, something dark that scared Mike even more than anything he'd seen in the military. It must have scared everyone else too, because they all just stood there. Then she turned and ran.

THERE WAS no way Emery was going to let Rachel get away with trying to kill her, Haley, and Kendra. She took off after Rachel without even thinking. She alone knew all the paths in the garden, so she'd have the best chance of catching her. She took off after the crazy bridesmaid while everyone else stood frozen, trying to process exactly what was going on.

Rachel had gone down the path near the oak tree. Emery knew a shortcut, so she zigged onto a smaller path, thinking she could head her off. But Rachel was too fast! She zoomed past right before Emery got to the fork.

"Stop!" Emery yelled, but it didn't even slow Rachel down.

Emery fell in behind her, willing her legs to go faster, her heart pumping. She heard the others following behind them and almost wished she hadn't given chase. She shouldn't have done it, because it would call attention to her, but she wouldn't be able to forgive herself if Rachel got away because she held back.

Up ahead the path split in several directions, some of them leading to the dense forest of the conservation land beside the inn. Rachel was incredibly fast. The girl must be a marathon runner or something. Too bad, because if she made it into the forest, she might get away.

Then, just before the path split, Angus—the little orange stray tabby—sprinted out of nowhere and directly across Rachel's path.

Rachel squeaked. Losing her footing, she tumbled headlong into the massive tangle of wild blackberry bushes. Emery hadn't gotten to this part of the garden yet and hadn't been able to trim them, so they were filled with prickly brambles. That turned out to be a good thing, because they held Rachel in place as she struggled to release herself from their thorny clutches.

Emery had skidded to a halt, and now some of the others piled up behind her.

They stood back and shook their heads at the sight of Rachel, cursing a blue streak and struggling to free herself from the branches and burrs that held her hostage. "Get me out of here! These things won't let me go!"

Sirens wailed from the front of the house, and soon they heard the police and fire department making their way into the part of the garden where the shed was.

"I'll run back and tell them we're down here," Mark said.

Mark ran off, and Todd and Aaron worked at freeing the still-struggling Rachel from the bush.

They were still working on it when Mark returned with two uniformed police officers.

"The shed?" Emery raised her brows at one of the officers. Even though the shed was old and needed to be replaced, she still used it for her tools. She hoped it wasn't a total loss, as those tools might be costly for Ginny to replace. Then again, Ginny was planning to replace the shed on her own dime, and the insurance money from the fire might outweigh the cost of new tools.

"It sustained a lot of damage. Won't be safe to use. But most of the tools made it through." One cop eyed Emery's soot-covered shirt as the other helped pull Rachel out. "Were you one of the victims of the fire?"

"Yes," Emery said.

"Me too." Kendra appeared at her side, casting cautious sidelong looks at Rachel.

"Right." He pulled out a notepad and pen. "Can you tell me what happened?"

As both Emery and Kendra recounted their stories for the officer, Rachel was extracted, put in handcuffs, and read her rights by the second cop.

"I didn't mean to hurt anybody," Rachel said, struggling against her bonds. "I only wanted to show Jared what a hero I am. To win him back."

"He's marrying me," Kendra said. "I thought you were my friend."

"How could I be friends with the woman who stole my man?" Rachel snarled. "I hate you."

"Sweetie, are you okay?" Jared stumbled up and took Kendra into his arms as Emery looked away.

Ughhh. Mushy stuff. Emery wasn't a fan of mushy stuff.

"I was so scared something happened to you. I don't know what I'd do if I lost you." Jared bent to kiss Kendra, and Rachel shrieked. "Don't kiss her. You love me. You've always loved me."

Jared turned and gave the crazy woman a flat look. "I never loved you, and I was always clear with you where we stood. I'm sorry you couldn't accept that. You need help, Rachel. Maybe now you'll finally get it."

More curses rang out as the officers led Rachel away, kicking and screaming.

Jared and Kendra kissed some more, and Emery turned away. Now that this was over, she just wanted to fade back into the gardens. Become invisible again. But as she started down the path, Mike and Haley came walking up hand in hand, looking even more mushy than Kendra and Jared. *Yech.*

"Emery, thank you for everything." Haley hugged her before she could stop it from happening. *Double yech.*

"I didn't do much. Just figured I knew the paths, so I gave chase."

Mike pulled Haley close. "I'm just glad none of you got hurt badly."

Emery smiled and skirted past them. It wasn't hard. They were so wrapped up in each other that neither one of them noticed her trying to fade into the background.

But it wasn't meant to be just yet. Another obstacle sat in the path in front of her. Angus. And he was licking his paw and wiping behind his ear nonchalantly, as if he hadn't just saved the day.

Emery bent to pick him up and cuddled him under her chin, her heart swelling at the loud purr he rewarded her with. "Don't worry, Angus, I know who the real hero is here, and I'm not going to forget it."

MIKE SAW Emery pick the orange tabby up out of the corner of his eye, but his full attention was on Haley. Even covered in soot and hacking like she was going to cough up a lung, Haley was still the most beautiful thing he'd ever seen.

He led her away down the path, further from the rest of the crowd, then turned her around to face him, slipping his arm around her waist. She placed her hand above his racing heart and blinked up at him, her mascara running, her eyes still red from the smoke.

"And thank you too," she said, her voice gravelly. "For saving us."

"My pleasure." He pulled her closer. "Thank you for putting up with a stubborn, scarred idiot like me."

She traced her fingers over the scars on his arm before bending to gently kiss each one. His battered heart melted, and what was left of his walls crumbled beneath her touch. "My pleasure."

Mike bent then and kissed her—gently, deeply, sweetly. When he pulled back at last, he smiled. "Are you sure you want to be with a guy like me? I'm not very pretty to look at anymore."

"Are you kidding?" she said, cupping his jaw tenderly. "I couldn't wish for a better man."

CHAPTER TWENTY-TWO

*I*n the end, the wedding started a few hours later than originally planned, but no one seemed to care. The weather was gorgeous, and the sunset was brilliant over the ocean as the minister pronounced Kendra and Jared man and wife. Even the old Firefly Inn glowed like a blushing bride on her wedding day, candles lit everywhere and tons of flowers and fresh garlands and lanterns strung from every bough.

From their places on opposite sides of the altar, Mike and Haley kept casting goofy, lovesick looks at each other, and Haley couldn't remember ever feeling happier in her life. Her sister's wedding was finally over, and Rachel was behind bars pending a hearing with the local judge that Monday.

Somehow, they'd even managed to talk Emery into

putting on Rachel's bridesmaid dress and stand in so the wedding party wouldn't be short a person. She looked about as thrilled as a pig on roasting day, but she'd done it nonetheless. She also looked beautiful, though she scoffed at any compliments thrown her way.

"You may now kiss the bride," the reverend said, and whoops and hollers went up as Kendra and Jared shared their first kiss as man and wife. Jared still looked a bit pale after his ordeal with the drugs Rachel had snuck into those sandwiches, but after a pot of coffee and a cold shower, he was back on his feet again and ready for holy matrimony.

As the crowd dispersed toward the patio where the reception dinner was set up, Haley couldn't help running through the past week in her mind. Looking back, all the clues had pointed to Rachel from the start, but for whatever reason, Haley hadn't connected the dots. Thankfully everything had worked out in the end. *More* than worked out if the way Mike was looking at her was any indication.

By the time Haley found her seat at the table, next to Mike of course, Jared was on his feet with a glass of champagne held high for a toast. "To my beautiful bride and her lovely sister. And to the fearless Emery, for battling the bad guys and making sure true love won in the end."

Kendra giggled, Haley shook her head and smiled, and Emery blushed and looked away—obviously shying away from his praise for her efforts. Dinner went to plan, too, with delicious filet mignon and duchess potatoes, glazed carrots, and fresh blueberry sorbet.

Stuffed and a bit sore after the day's grueling activities, Haley sat back in her chair to watch the other couples dance around the wooden floor they'd set up just off the patio in a grassy open area of the gardens. The waning light showcased the backdrop of the ocean, turning it bright aqua and pink. The whole scene was punctuated by the magical flickering lights of the fireflies in the darker area of the garden as they weaved around the trees in lazy paths as if they'd been hired to add the ambiance.

A DJ played all of Kendra and Jared's favorites. Mike stayed by Haley's side, his arm draped over the back of her chair and his fingers tracing lazy patterns on her bare shoulder.

"Do you want to dance?" he asked, his warm breath on her ear causing her to shiver.

"Nah, I'm good." She snuggled into his side and took his hand. "Better than good, actually."

"Yeah?" He leaned over and kissed her quickly before settling back in his seat. "We'll have some figuring out to do once we get back home again."

"True." She stared down at their joined fingers in her lap. "Will doing the long-distance thing for a while be a problem for you?"

"I travel all the time for work, so what's a couple hundred more miles a week." He chuckled, low and deep, and she felt that sound all the way to her toes. "Besides, if it's you I get to see at the end of my drive, it'll all be worth it."

"Aw, that's so sweet." She kissed his jaw. "And I can drive up to Sioux Falls too. It's not fair you have to do all the traveling. I want this to work out between us, so it has to be equal."

"Agreed." He smiled. "I want this to work out too."

"Well, that's half the battle right there then." She had just leaned in to kiss him again when someone yelled, "Look out! Incoming!"

Haley glanced over to see Kendra's bouquet flying right for her and Mike. But at the last second, a gust of wind blew, knocking the bouquet sideways and straight into Emery's hands. The poor girl looked astounded and was handling the bouquet like a hot potato that she couldn't wait to pass off to someone else.

That must have been one strong gust of wind. Haley had never seen one blow something as heavy as a bouquet before. Then again, she'd seen a lot of things at the Firefly Inn that seemed impossible. Haley snorted and shrugged. "Guess that one's a goner."

"I wouldn't worry," Mike said, bending his head until their lips were just a breath apart. "I don't think you need to catch a bouquet to know you might be the next one getting married."

GINNY WATCHED the proceedings through the conservatory windows. After a week full of guests, she was ready for a little break. Relief and exhaustion swept through her. It was over. Finally. And in the end, it had all worked out beautifully.

Over the cliffs, the last of the sun's rays shone in vibrant hues of scarlet and gold, and she couldn't help thinking about her Donald. Now that she was busier, she dwelled on his memory less and less, which was probably a good thing. The pain around her heart when she pictured his face had lessened too—also good.

"Meow."

The plaintive sound drew her attention downward to see the tiny orange tabby from the garden. The large French doors in the conservatory were open, and he must've wandered in while the reception was in full swing outside.

"Yes, I did hear that you helped catch the bad guy." Ginny looked down at his empty bowl. She'd already given him a treat—a large piece of filet—for his bravery. "Don't get used to the treats though."

He slitted one eye as he scowled at her. "Mew."

"Nice try. Things are looking up around here, though, eh, Angus?" she said, smiling as the cat stopped scowling and started purring. Absently, she bent and stroked his little head, talking to him like he was a person. Then she realized what she was doing and quickly pulled away. "Hopefully this is the first of many more successful events."

"Indeed, madam. Indeed." Dooley's disembodied voice rumbled through the air around her, lifting the tiny hairs on the back of Ginny's neck and causing the cat to screech and dart away into the shadows of the room.

She glanced around her wide-eyed. Had that been her imagination? No one outside seemed to have heard a thing. Just Ginny and the cat. Still, she'd not missed the way that bouquet had suddenly changed direction mid-flight. Nor had she forgotten all those candles lighting at once the night the power went out.

"Dooley?" she asked into thin air.

"Of course. Who else did you expect?"

Ginny sat in the chair, stunned. Was she actually talking to a ghost? "What do you want?"

But Dooley didn't answer. Ginny held her breath, waiting, the ticking of the grandfather clock competing with the thud of her heartbeat, but no answer ever came.

She sighed and started out of the conservatory, heading back to the kitchen. Well, if there was a ghost in the house, at least he seemed friendly enough, and he *had* helped her when she needed it. Couldn't argue with that.

Still, as she walked back into the kitchen, Ginny double-checked to make sure those salt shakers were exactly where she'd promised Dooley they'd be—on the window sill.

****

More Books in the Firefly Inn Series:
Another Chance (Book 1)

GET emails for all of Meredith Summers latest women's fiction sweet romances:

https://lee-83c5.gr8.com

ALSO BY MEREDITH SUMMERS

Lobster Bay Series:

Saving Sandcastles (Book 1)

Changing Tides (Book 2)

Making Waves (Book 3)

Shifting Sands (Book 4)

Shell Cove Series:

Beachcomber Motel (Book 1)

ALSO BY ANNIE DOBBS

Sweet Romance

Firefly Inn Series

***

Another Chance (Book 1)

Another Wish (Book 2)

Sweet Mountain Billionaires

***

Jaded Billionaire (Book 1)

Billionaire Backlash (Book 2)

Hometown Hearts Series

***

No Getting Over You (Book 1)

A Change of Heart (Book 2)

Magical Romance with a Touch of Mystery

***

Something Magical

Curiously Enchanted

****

Romance and Cozy Mystery - Written as Leighann Dobbs:

Romantic Comedy

***

Corporate Chaos Series

In Over Her Head (book 1)

Can't Stand the Heat (book 2)

Contemporary Romance

***

Reluctant Romance

Cozy Mysteries

Lexy Baker

Cozy Mystery Series

* * *

Lexy Baker Cozy Mystery Series Boxed Set Vol 1 (Books 1-4)

Or buy the books separately:

Killer Cupcakes

Dying For Danish

Murder, Money and Marzipan

3 Bodies and a Biscotti

Brownies, Bodies & Bad Guys

Bake, Battle & Roll

Wedded Blintz

Scones, Skulls & Scams

Ice Cream Murder

Mummified Meringues

Brutal Brulee (Novella)

No Scone Unturned

Cream Puff Killer

Mooseamuck Island

Cozy Mystery Series

* * *

A Zen For Murder

A Crabby Killer

A Treacherous Treasure

Mystic Notch

Cat Cozy Mystery Series

* * *

Ghostly Paws

A Spirited Tail

A Mew To A Kill

Paws and Effect

Probable Paws

Silver Hollow

Paranormal Cozy Mystery Series

***

A Spell of Trouble (Book 1)

Spell Disaster (Book 2)

Nothing to Croak About (Book 3)

Cry Wolf (Book 4)

Blackmoore Sisters

Cozy Mystery Series

* * *

Dead Wrong

Dead & Buried

Dead Tide

Buried Secrets

Deadly Intentions

A Grave Mistake

Spell Found

Fatal Fortune

Western Historical Romance

***

Goldwater Creek Mail Order Brides:

Faith

American Mail Order Brides Series:

Chevonne: Bride of Oklahoma

ABOUT MEREDITH SUMMERS

Meredith Summers writes cozy mysteries as USA Today Bestselling author Leighann Dobbs and crime fiction as L. A. Dobbs.

She spent her childhood summers in Ogunquit Maine and never forgot the soft soothing feeling of the beach. She hopes to share that feeling with you through her books which are all light, feel-good reads.

Join her newsletter for sneak peeks of the latest books and release day notifications:

https://lobsterbay1.gr8.com

Made in the USA
Las Vegas, NV
31 October 2023

80032215R00133